HIS PERMANENT SCAR

THE BRIDES OF PURPLE HEART RANCH BOOK 4

SHANAE JOHNSON

THOSE JOHNSON GIRLS

*D*ust kicked up the gravel as the yellow school bus pulled up the drive to the Bellflower Ranch. Though no one called this place by that name. All the residents and inhabitants had christened the sprawling land the Purple Heart Ranch due to the wounded warriors who came there to find healing both inside and out.

Sean Jeffries watched the bus as it came to a stop beside the mess hall. The hall was a converted barn where the veterans took their meals. Well, those veterans who weren't married took their meals in the barn. The number of single men on the ranch was dwindling fast. Only two were left, and Sean was one of them.

Pretty soon there would be no single men

residing on this ranch. The zoning regulation that deemed the ranch could only be inhabited by family members was due to take effect at the end of the month. When that day came, both Sean and the other last single soldier standing, Xavier Ramos, would have to hightail it off the land. It was a day Sean was not looking forward to. But there was nothing he could do about it. He had no plans to get married anytime soon, if ever.

Instead of thinking about his own fate, Sean focused on the future of the ranch. That future was stepping out of the school bus. One by one, the scraggly boys hopped off the bus. Some had wide eyes as they looked around the ranch. Others had narrowed gazes filled with suspicion. Some formed groups and stood close. A few others stood apart and solitary.

Sean didn't blame either group of boys. It wasn't how he'd looked his first day of basic training for the army. He'd been entirely trusting of his superiors, of his fellow soldiers, of the entire process. That trust had served him well in training. But when he'd finally gotten out into the field and right into the trenches of war, that training had failed him and nearly taken the lives of his brothers at arms.

The sun glared down at him in the afternoon sky.

Sean slunk back into the shadows of the barn. Being in the spotlight, having the heat of the sun on him, brought back the nightmares of the explosion. With his eyes wide open, he saw the horrors of that day played out again.

Men working together to build a school for their community. Women offering aid to give their families a brighter future. Children running around in excitement at opportunities they would soon be receiving. And one child standing off to the side with a secret that would send it all crashing down.

Sean clenched his fists. His hands were empty of his weapon. He'd laid down his weapons after his mistake that day and hadn't armed himself since. He also kept his distance from strangers in general, but innocent-looking children in particular.

At his side, Scar sat on her rump breathing heavily in the midday sun. The pug scratched at her skin, her nails gnawing at the missing patches of fur on her back. A couple of the other ranch dogs waited eagerly for the new humans to step off the bus, likely hoping to get new playmates. But Star was a cautious little beast. She'd been scorned one too many times by humans to trust them immediately.

The kids that came off the bus were mostly black and brown. They were all from the same inner city neighborhood. Sean's childhood neighborhood hadn't been so homogenous. He'd grown up in a racially and culturally diverse neighborhood; the true American Dream where people who'd come from money and people who'd bootstrapped themselves up to success lived in relative harmony. Much like the veterans who occupied the ranch and were now extending a helping hand to these boys in need.

"Welcome to the Purple Heart Ranch," said Francisco Demonti. "You twelve have been chosen to participate in our youth program because you're having some trouble at school. That could be trouble with grades, trouble with social interactions, trouble with authority, or all three."

Since the ranch opened a year ago to rehabilitate wounded soldiers, this had been a dream of Fran's and Dylan's. Neither had been a troubled kid in their youths. Sean suspected that both meant they were subconsciously gearing these kids toward a life in the service.

Even with the scars they'd all gained, the limbs they'd sacrificed, and the friends they'd lost, Sean did not regret his time in the service. The U.S. Military had made him the man he was; a man with loyalty and honor. A man who knew that not all militaries held the same values and could make monsters out of men.

Sean also knew that it didn't have to be a government-run army that could turn men and young boys onto the wrong path. Some streets in America were meaner than those in Syria and Afghanistan. Better these kids went into the service than get caught up in a street gang.

But the kids weren't listening to Fran. Their attention was diverted elsewhere. Two men rode up on horses.

When they got to the gathered group of boys, Dylan swung his prosthetic leg over the horse and climbed down. Beside him, Reed Cannon also dismounted. When his feet struck the ground, he kept his prosthetic hand on the reigns to the mare.

"Man, this is a place for cripples," he heard one kid stage whisper loud enough to be certain he was heard.

Sean hung back in the shadows with Star. The pug looked up at him with her scarred face. The dog had a face that only a mother could love. The same could be said about Sean. Sean reached down and gave the dog a scratch under her chin to reassure her. The dog lolled her tongue in ecstasy at the gesture.

Sean didn't patronize the dog by telling her it was what was on the inside the mattered. Sean knew all too well that people judged the outside first and often didn't make it to look at someone's character.

"Look at the dogs," another boy snickered and pointed.

Soldier, the three-legged Chihuahua, and Spin the wheelchair-bound Irish Terrier sat panting, waiting eagerly for the go-ahead to mingle amongst the boys and make new friends.

"Yo, man, check out Quasimodo over there," said another of the boys. His stubby finger was pointed into the shadows at Sean.

Sean had to give the kid props. At least he knew his literature. Sean was a disfigured man lurking in the shadows. The scar on his face was a souvenir from his time in service, just like Dylan's missing leg, Reed's missing arm, and the shrapnel buried in Fran's chest.

Fran whistled loud to get the kids' attention. The boys didn't all straighten their backs, lift their heads, and stand tall as a soldier would when called to attention. But they did quiet down and turn their gazes over to Fran.

Fran didn't address the boys' comments with words. Like all the soldiers on this ranch, Fran was a man of action. He would show these kids the meaning of the word respect, likely in the horse stalls.

A small smile cracked Sean's lips at the thought of what Fran had in store for them. But as he smiled, his skin pulled and tugged and rippled uncomfortably. His scar limited his ability to express himself, which was fine since there were few people Sean wanted to show emotion to.

When he turned to head in the opposite direction of the group, he came face to face with one of the kids. The boy could have been a smaller version of himself. The kid stood back in the shadows. His shoulders were hunched to be unassuming. His body language said stay back, I'm not friendly.

"Does he bite?" the kid asked.

It took Sean a moment to realize he wasn't asking if Sean bit. The kid was asking about the dog. Star lifted her nose and gave the kid a tentative sniff. The pug must have found the kid to be okay because she reached out her tongue and gave the kid's hand a lick. That answered the kid's question.

Star was entirely docile. She just looked mean because of her smooshed mug and the patches of skin missing from her back. But give the dog a scratch behind the ear, show her a bit of kindness, and she would be your devoted friend for life.

"Aren't you supposed to be with the others?" Sean asked the boy.

The kid shrugged as he scratched Star's ears. He opened his mouth to speak but a fit of coughs came out instead. "I have allergies."

That didn't sound like allergies to Sean. The cough was too deep. The kid struggled for breath as the fit overtook him.

"How long have you had that cough?" asked Sean.

The kid shrugged. "Couple weeks maybe?"

"Have you been to the doctor?"

"We can't afford health insurance. My dad says it'll go away once the seasons change."

A whistle sounded from across the way. Sean, Star and the kid stood to attention at the call of Fran's whistle. Fran motioned to the boy.

The kid sighed, clearly wanting to hang with the dog more than he wanted to go and join the other humans. He gave Star one more pat. Without so much as a nod to Sean, he turned to go to the others. But before he took his first step, another series of coughs wracked his body. Once he caught his breath, he made his way over.

Sean almost stopped him, but he let the kid go. It wasn't his responsibility. The kid's parent would take care of it. Or not.

Sean would never be responsible for another child, or another soul. After facing off with a child soldier back in Afghanistan, he was happy to stay away from children for the rest of his life.

CHAPTER TWO

Contrary to her family and friends' beliefs, Ruhi Patel believed in love. Love was a scientific, provable fact. Beyond the data, she'd experienced it happen many times with her own five senses.

She'd seen it in her father's glances at her mother. She'd smelled it in the food her brother, Kabir, cooked for his wife, tasted it in the curries her sister-in-law made for her extended family. Ruhi had heard it in the songs her sister, Anika, sang for her husband. But Ruhi had never felt it herself.

And that was fine. Ruhi wasn't looking for love. Not exactly. She was far too practical and grounded. But she did harbor a hope that, like her parents and siblings who'd all fallen in love at first sight, love would sneak up on her and knock her off her feet.

"Ruhi, we have to talk."

Those words certainly knocked Ruhi back on her feet. But it was in the wrong direction. It wasn't what she was expecting to hear from the guy she'd been seeing for the past five months.

Ruhi had been spending most weekends at Dr. Michael Paskiewicz's place. So, this talk could go either way. Either he wanted to end the relationship or he wanted to move it forward.

They were seated in a small cafe in the trendy district in town. It was a place just outside the free clinic they both worked in; she as a nurse practitioner and he as a doctor. The entire clinic often came to this place before their shift started to get a mug of dark brewed energy, or for lunch to get refueled with a protein-packed sandwich.

It was after work now and Ruhi was having a tuna salad. Admittedly, it wasn't the best choice while on a date, and her stomach had grumbled a bit at the choice. But she and Michael were past the impress-me stage. The trouble was she didn't know if they were moving on up from there or taking a detour to a dead end.

Ruhi leaned back in her chair. For the first time

in a long time, she considered; What did she want? Did she want to progress or get off this ride with Michael? And if they did progress, how far was she willing to go?

She'd always proclaimed she wouldn't get married or have a family until her career was well underway. She wasn't exactly where she wanted to be with her career today. Her soul was satisfied helping the less fortunate at the free clinic, as well as working with wounded veterans alongside her father at the Purple Heart Ranch. Still, there was more she wanted to do.

She'd applied to work with Doctors Without Borders, an organization that provided medical aid where it was most needed and often not accessible. It had always been her dream to travel and offer her services to those who needed it most. Unfortunately, she was still waiting to hear back about her application to the organization. If she got the job, it wouldn't be conducive to a relationship.

"We've been seeing each other for four months now ..." Michael was saying.

It was actually five. But who could expect the guy in the relationship to keep track? Michael probably wasn't counting their first few weeks of dating. Or all the times when they'd gone out in a group but stuck close to one another.

"... and I think you feel it too."

It? Did she feel *it*? She supposed she felt something for him. And apparently, he felt something too.

He didn't reach across the table for her hands. He retracted both of his hands below the table. Ruhi looked down and saw a bulge in his pocket.

This was it. He was going to do it. He was going to propose ... something. That they move in together? That they join their assets? That they get engaged?

Her gaze stuck to the bulge. Was it big enough to be a ring? Or maybe a spare key? No, it was too fat to be a key. It had to be a ring.

Oh, God. It was happening. She was getting proposed to. But did she want to be proposed to? Did she love him? Did love truly matter in these days?

She and Michael were entirely compatible. Even though everyone in her family had fallen in love at first sight, they'd all had their unions arranged based on compatibility. Her parents were matched based on their personalities and goals. Kabir and his wife were both in the food industry and loved classic literature. Anika was a singer and her husband wrote film scores.

Ruhi and Michael were both in the same field. They were both health conscious and environmentally responsible. He had a compost bin and a rain barrel in the back of his townhouse, which was seriously sexy. And he drove a Prius.

Dr. Michael Paskiewicz was perfect for her in every way. She would be a fool not to say yes to his proposal.

Michael tilted his gaze up to hers, and suddenly, she felt it. That *it*. The butterflies in her stomach. But they felt a bit more like bees buzzing around and stinging her.

She felt some of the fish bubble up in her throat as though it wanted to break free. Oh, no! Was she about to barf?

She couldn't. Not now. She had to hold it in. This would not make for a great story to tell their children about how daddy proposed to mommy.

"Yeah, I can see you feel it too," said Michael. "There's just not that spark between us."

Ruhi blinked. She opened her mouth ... and burped.

Michael reared back. He wrinkled his nose. She'd had extra onions on her sandwich, so not only did he get a whiff of the sea, he got the pungent smell of an earthy weed.

Ruhi's hands shot to her mouth, and she caught a whiff herself. But the embarrassment of her bad breath paled in comparison to the embarrassment of her assumption. "You're breaking up with me?"

"Breaking up?" Michael's nose relaxed and his brows pinched. "We weren't exactly a couple. Were we? I just thought we were hanging out. Being casual. Isn't that what you said you wanted?"

It had been what she said. Five months ago. But by the third month, she'd assumed they were a couple. Who wouldn't have?

"I feel that we're better off as just friends," he said.

Translation: *I don't want to commit to you but I'd still like to come over in the middle of the night on a weekday if that's cool.*

"I'm going to take some time and work on myself," he said.

Translation: *I'm going to go off and be selfish and self-centered and everyone else can take a hike because I won't notice.*

"It's not you, it's me."

Translation: *It was totally her, and he didn't want to see her anymore.*

"We're on different paths," he said.

Translation: *You're a slacker, and I'm about to climb a rung up the ladder of success and leave you in the basement.*

Michael reached in his pocket and pulled out the thick bulge. It wasn't a key. It wasn't a ring. It was an envelope. He pulled out a piece of paper.

"See? I got accepted to Doctors Without Borders."

Ruhi's stomach twisted the knot it had tied itself into in the other direction. "I didn't know you applied."

"I got interested when you talked about it. I applied on a whim, and I got in. I leave in a week."

"Wow. That's just ..."

Not only was he dumping her after their casual, five-month-long, exclusive relationship. Wait? Had he been monogamous?

She couldn't ask now. She wouldn't get a key or a ring, and he was stealing her dream job. Her stomach untwisted, and she lurched again. Her hand covered her mouth in time, and she tasted bile. She had to get out of there.

"We'll still be friends, right?" said Michael.

That was the last straw. There was a votive candle on the table between them. Ruhi picked up her water glass and tossed it in his face. It doused the candle and the rest of the tuna sandwich. But mostly it soaked Michael's face and his shirt.

"Oh, my bad," she said standing up. "Thought I saw a spark."

And with that, she marched out of the restaurant without looking back. She made it all the way to the alley before bending over and giving up her meal to a gutter.

CHAPTER THREE

Sean rode the horse at a gallop. It was the only time in the world he felt free, in command.

He'd driven tanks in the army. He'd been in foxholes waiting for insurgents to appear. He'd jumped out of helicopters and into danger zones. None of that compared to commanding a horse.

The feel of the wind biting his face made him forget about the tug of the scars when he smiled. It was the only time he smiled, because the feel of the wind on his face negated the tug of the scars on his cheek.

Equine therapy had given Sean back his life. That and the healing touch of a certain nurse practitioner. But Sean could ride horses every day.

He could only see Nurse Ruhi on their appointed days, and he could never tell her how he felt about her. He was sure her professional relationship prohibited her from dating any of her patients. But besides that, Ruhi was seeing someone else.

Dr. Pasteurizer, as Sean had dubbed him, appeared to be the perfect partner for Ruhi. But something about the man had always rubbed Sean the wrong way. The few times the man had been on the ranch helping out, he'd never looked directly at the people in his care. He was one of those doctors who focused on the charts and not the patient. Where Ruhi always insisted Sean hold his head high and look her in the eye when he was under her care.

It was the main thing Sean would miss about the ranch. When he moved off the ranch next month, he would have to change health care providers. He knew Ruhi worked at a free clinic, but the government took far too good care of him to qualify for those services, and Sean would never take away a spot from those in need.

So, after next month, he'd only see Ruhi in passing when he visited the ranch. Or when he managed to catch her at her family's restaurant. He'd gone to her apartment for her birthday a couple of months ago, but that had been as a group with the others.

He was certain he couldn't just show up there to hang out and have to tilt his chin up so that she could look at his cheek as she examined him, see in his eyes as he answered her questions.

He had no inclination to marry anyone else to stay on the ranch and continue to see her. It wouldn't be right to offer his hand to someone else when another woman held his heart. And Sean knew Ruhi wasn't interested in his heart, only his healing.

Which was enough. It had to be. He brought the horse to a trot as he saw signs of others up ahead.

In the distance, he saw the young boys of the after-school program. They were split into two groups. One boy in each group was blindfolded and wandering around.

It was a trust game from his army days. It was designed to teach the team members to watch each other's back and keep them out of harm's way.

The coughing boy was one of the two who wore a blindfold. At the moment, he was headed into a pile of firewood. No one from his group was warning him. Instead, the boys of his team were covering their mouths to keep from laughing too loud.

Standing off to the side, Dylan watched it all go

down. The Sergeant did not look happy. But neither did he intervene. Sean knew a hard lesson was about to be learned.

As expected, the kid walked into the pile and fell. The others around him tore their hands from their mouths and burst out laughing.

The kid tore off the blindfold. His dark face was screwed with confusion, and then betrayal, and then anger. He got up and raced for one of the bigger boys. The smaller kid tackled the big kid to the ground before Dylan could intervene.

Both kids were out of breath as they were separated. The little kid coughed and kept coughing. Then he doubled over and coughed a bit more, struggling for breath. They all waited for the kid to right himself. When he did, it was clear the fight was far from over.

"This team is on stable duty," announced Dylan.

The boys groaned. Sean would've too. Cleaning out the horses' stables was his least favorite job on the ranch.

"You did not have your brother's back," Dylan continued. "You work together as a unit and succeed. Or you all fail. If one man falls, you all do."

Dylan turned to the little cougher. "What's your name, kid?"

"James."

"And yours?" Dylan turned to the kid who'd taken the hit.

"Maurice."

"Maurice, take James to go see the nurse."

"I'm fine," wheezed James. Then he gulped down air before launching into another coughing fit.

The kids weren't laughing anymore. In fact, Maurice's face was screwed up in worry. He turned to Dylan.

"I don't know where the nurse is?"

"I'll show him," said Sean. He handed the horse's reins to Dylan and motioned for the kids to follow.

"I don't need his help," James managed between coughs.

"Look, I'm sorry," said Maurice. "I thought it was funny. Don't take it so serious."

"Whatever," said James. Then he turned to Sean. "The cough isn't serious. It's just allergies."

That was not allergies. Sean had no patience to entertain the kid. He pointed them both in the direction he wanted them to head toward. The medical suite where Ruhi was on duty today.

The other kid, Maurice, was ready to turn on his heel and head back to join the group. But before he did, he caught Sean's gaze. The judgment in Sean's eyes must've turned him around.

"Come on," Maurice said to James. "Let's go."

"I said you don't have to come with me. I don't need your pity."

"I gave the Sergeant my word. Whether you like it or not, I'm gonna do what I said."

Part of Sean wanted to cheer the kid. The other part of him wanted to roll his eyes. But it was a start. He marched behind the two as they headed into the medical suite. The walked past Dr. Patel's offices and straight to the back where Ruhi's exam room was tucked.

Sean listened to hear if she was in with another patient, but he knew she wasn't. He likely knew her schedule better than her planner. She had no appointments at this time unless someone came in with an injury. And there was silence coming from the room. Only the scratch-scratching of a pencil against a clipboard.

But as he drew nearer, that sound stopped abruptly. It was followed by a heaving sound, as though someone was about to be sick. Sean stepped in front of the two boys to get into the room.

And there she was. The sight of her was always a blow to his solar plexus. But this blow went straight to his gut. Ruhi was leaning over the sink, rubbing her stomach and grimacing.

"You okay?" Sean said coming into the room and standing by her side.

"Just something I ate." Ruhi straightened and pulled on a smile.

Sean's mouth itched to do the same. Aside from being on a horse, she was the only one who could elicit a grin from him. Even when she was on the cusp of being sick, she made his heart beat faster.

Sean was used to sensing and containing danger. But whenever he was around her, he only felt peace. He didn't know how he'd manage without that constant smile in his life.

"What can I do for you guys?" she asked, looking past him at the boys.

Before Sean could speak, James started coughing again.

"That does not sound good," said Ruhi.

"It's my fault," said Maurice. He stepped forward as though physically taking responsibility. "I played a joke, and he fell down and hurt himself."

Ruhi shook her head. "That's not a fall down cough. That sounds like there's fluid in your lungs."

She motioned James into the room and began her examination. Sean took the opportunity to openly gaze at her. Her golden skin looked a bit sallow today. There were slight bags under her eyes as though she'd either been crying or not sleeping well. There were no jokes or attempts at light-hearted banter in her conversation with James. The air about her, which was usually charged with electric energy, felt depleted.

Something was wrong. Maybe she was sick? She looked a little green around the gills.

"It's bronchitis," Ruhi pronounced sometime later.

"Is it my fault?" asked Maurice. Remorse was clear in his eyes.

"No, sweetie," said Ruhi. "It's an infection. James will be fine so long as he takes care of himself. He'll need some medicine."

"So, I'll have to stay home from school and the ranch?" James asked. To Sean's surprise, he did not seem happy about the option of a day off from school.

"No, if you're up to it, you can go to school, and you can come to the ranch. You just have to take it easy. You're going to feel tired a lot."

"But I won't be able to participate in the activities?" James asked. "I'll be a drag on the team?"

"Not if you have help," said Sean. He looked to Maurice.

"I'll help," said Maurice.

"I don't need you to," wheezed James. He hopped off the exam bed and squared off against Maurice.

"Well, you're on my team, so I have to." Maurice met him toe to toe.

With a sigh, Sean got between the two. With a stern look from him, they both backed down. Ruhi tore a piece of paper from her prescription pad.

"Give this prescription to your mom," said Ruhi.

"My mom isn't with us." The kid looked away as he said it.

The way he said it made Sean think that his mom was alive, just not physically present. She could be in jail, rehab, or skipped out on him entirely.

"Your dad?"

James nodded. He took the note from Ruhi, holding it carefully as though it were expensive lace. "How much is it gonna cost?"

"It's not too expensive," said Ruhi. "If you're dad needs help paying I know some charitable organizations who will help."

"We're not a charity case."

Looking at the kid's clothes, Sean begged to

differ. He was also smaller than the other kids his age. Sean wondered if the kid had been born addicted to drugs?

James folded the piece of paper and shoved it in his pocket. With a hunch of his shoulders, he headed out of the room. Maurice waited a couple of steps and then trailed after him.

Sean turned to Ruhi. "Should we call social services?"

"What for?"

"He said earlier he's been coughing for a couple of weeks. His parents might be neglecting him."

"Let's keep an eye on the situation first," she said. "We don't know the whole story."

"My parents would've rushed me to the hospital at the first cough."

"Your parents could afford it and had the resources."

Ruhi lifted her hand to pat Sean on his back. But her hand wavered. Instead of landing on his back, she put it to her belly. And then to her mouth.

"Ruhi?"

But she dashed away from him and back to the sink in the back of the room. Ruhi doubled over. Her body was wracked by retching sounds. Sean made it to her in time to gather her hair from her face and hold it away from the sickness that overtook her.

"I'm fine," she choked out.

But she didn't sound fine. Aside from a bit of sick on her face, there were also tears streaming down her cheeks. Despite still looking beautiful, she was most definitely not fine.

CHAPTER FOUR

This could not be happening. No. This was not happening.

Ruhi's stomach disagreed with her as it squeezed out the orange juice she'd drank that morning. But no, even that small bit of citrus was gone. Only bile coated her tongue.

This was not food poisoning as she'd hoped. That tuna salad sandwich that she'd thrown up yesterday was long gone from her system. So she knew it wasn't that.

She couldn't bring herself to say what it could be. Instead, she did what any medical professional would do. She went through the symptoms.

Her bra irritated her, and her breasts were super sensitive. She'd been visiting the bathroom more times than she cared to count over the last few days. She was tired as soon as she woke up, and she'd closed her office door to take a nap twice this week. There was also the nausea without vomiting. And the last two days of nausea with the vomiting.

All those symptoms could point to the flu. Or pneumonia. Possibly mononucleosis. Even meningitis. Oh, how she wished she had meningitis.

But the calendar didn't lie. Ruhi was almost a week late for her monthly visitor. She was never late. Not since her first visit at the ripe age of twelve. Her body was like clockwork. Still, she couldn't give her diagnosis voice.

How had this happened? She'd been careful. She was always careful. But contraceptives weren't foolproof. There was always a slim chance. How had she beaten the only odds she didn't want to?

"Ruhi?"

Sean's voice sounded behind her. He'd pulled her hair from her face as she'd lost the contents of her stomach, just like a good girlfriend would do. But Sean was a grown man, and he'd seen her puke in the sink. Would embarrassment leave her alone for a just a day?

"I'm fine."

She closed her eyes as she tried to straighten.

She didn't want to see her reflection in the mirror. She didn't want to see herself like this. She didn't want anyone to see her like this.

But she wasn't fine. Her stomach told the truth and twisted. She retched over the sink again, more bile leaving her body.

Her eyes opened as she came up for air. But she didn't see herself. The first thing she saw was Sean's scar. The angry gash wrinkled his brown skin.

And just like that, she suddenly craved a Hershey bar. Then the thought of any food made her sick, and she retched again. Only this time, instead of bile, tears rolled down her face. She was too tired to hide, and she let them flow.

Sean's hand came to her back. It was the first time he'd ever touched her. She'd touched him multiple times over the past year as she'd treated him. The feel of his hand at her back instantly calmed her stomach, but it made her feel even more tired. She had the urge to curl up in his arms and go to sleep. To let him hold her and shut the world out.

Ruhi straightened her back. She was not that type of girl. To lean on a man? No, thank you. Look at what that had gotten her.

"I'm fine," she insisted. But the moment she left

the comfort of Sean's arms her stomach protested again, and she turned back to the sink.

When she was done, too tired to hold her body weight, she slumped down onto the floor. The cool ceramic tile was nice on her skin. But even nicer was the feeling of Sean's fingers moving up and down her spine as he sat beside her.

Ruhi leaned her forehead against his shoulder. And they sat like that for long moments. In silence. Sean had never been much for words. His smiles were hard to come by, but he always had one for her.

"Should I get your father?" he asked.

"No."

That was the last thing she needed. Her parents were proud of her professionally. But she knew they worried about her in her social life. They were all smiles with each academic or career advancement. But with each new relationship, those prideful smiles slipped. With this news, she was certain she'd get alarmed looks and frowns.

What was she going to do? Being a single mother had never been in her plans. Her father would insist that Michael handle his responsibility. But Michael had already made it clear where his priorities lay. He was likely packing his bags, and maybe even bagging some other girl right now.

No. She would do this on her own. She'd tell Michael about the baby, of course. But not until she had everything figured out and well in hand first.

"Why don't you come lie down on one of the exam beds?" Sean offered.

"I'm fine. Just something that disagreed with me."

Sean's eyes said he didn't believe her. He was a watchful one. He always saw more than he let on beneath that hooded gaze of his. But Ruhi knew he'd never give voice to any suspicions.

"I'm fine," she insisted. "I'm going to be fine."

Sean brushed a stray piece of her hair back behind her ear. He offered her one of his small smiles. Ruhi's breath caught. She knew he was handsome, but she'd never looked at him that way. She was always more concerned about his healing.

The skin on his cheek wrinkled and Ruhi knew it pained him to do so. She had the urge to brush her thumb across that skin to smooth it out. But she didn't.

Sean pulled his hand back as though it had made the move on its own. "Is there someone else you want me to call?"

Ruhi closed her eyes. Though he didn't say it

exactly, it was clear Sean suspected what was truly going on inside her. Soon everyone would.

Ruhi had spoken of Michael. He'd been to the ranch a couple of times to pick her up or drop her off. He'd even consulted on a case or two. She knew that was the someone Sean was referring to when he asked if she wanted him to call someone.

"No, I don't want to talk to him."

Sean's gentle face transformed in an instant. As a soldier, a man of action, he might assume that violence had entered the picture.

"No," Ruhi held up her hands. "It's not like that. We broke up."

Sean's brow raised. Then his gaze lowered, looking pointedly at her flat belly.

Ruhi closed her eyes, unwilling to deal with the reality. "Sean, please. Just, please."

"Should I call your father?" he said again.

"Oh, God, no." Ruhi shuddered. When she did her face snuggled deeper into the nook of Sean's shoulder. Lifting her head felt like such a chore that she decided to simply stay there.

"Okay," he said. "Whatever you need."

Sean shifted and Ruhi heard the sound of water running. A cool cloth touched her mouth and she sank even deeper into Sean's embrace.

"Whatever you need."

Ruhi leaned into him as he pressed the cloth to her face. She wasn't sure how long they stayed like that. But the soothing, cool warmth was exactly what she needed.

CHAPTER FIVE

The feel of the heat on his back was real. But just like in reality, Sean knew he had to push forward. He had to find Xavier and get him out of danger.

It was just a dream. Sean knew he was dreaming, but that didn't stop the nightmares from tormenting him, trapping him in the darkness and making him relive the gruesome explosion over and over again.

The sounds of children crying deafened his ears. The sound of women wailing pierced his conscious. He had to duck as the bricks they'd laid earlier fell all around him. He had to watch his step as the splintering of wood that gave up the fight and joined the raging flame.

There were so many bodies around him. Some

called for help, but he couldn't get to them. Others were silent and still. But their accusations rang loud.

This was Sean's fault. It had happened on his watch. If he could take back that one second of hesitation ... would he?

No matter his choice, the kid would always die.

The smell of burning flesh, the screams that were shrill and then instantly muted like a radio being turned off, Sean pushed through it all to find Xavier. Dylan and Fran had been outside when the suicide bomber had depressed his weapon. After his second of hesitation and the worst had happened, Sean had sprung into action.

He'd managed to get Reed out and to safety while others worked on his injury. But when Sean did a head count of his unit, he hadn't seen Xavier. He'd only heard Xavier call out that there was danger. And then his friend was gone.

Sean had to wade through the wreckage of brick, wood, and bodies. He had to watch the light go out of the eyes of people he knew he couldn't save. All because he had looked into the once innocent eyes of a child and hesitated.

In the dream, he found Xavier as he'd done in reality. Xavier had been lying face down. Flames encroached in on him, preparing to consume him as they had the school that had been filled with hopes and dreams. The fire's heat had already licked off the back of Xavier's shirt. When Sean touched his back to grab hold of him, the man woke and screamed and started swinging from the pain of the burns.

Sean fell back into the wreckage. A piece of metal slapped him in the face, leaving a mark to forever remind him of that day and what war could do to the most innocent of human beings.

Sean and Xavier managed to get out before the building collapsed around them. But the smell stayed with Sean. The sounds stayed with him. And the scar would never let him forget.

It had been a child who'd done this. Just a boy of thirteen, radicalized by his father and sent off to become a weapon of war. That morning, a father had strapped a bomb to his son's body and sent him off to certain death, while he'd stayed behind.

There had been a tear in the boy's eye before he'd done what his father told him to do. It was the tear that made Sean pause in his perch.

Just last week, Sean had played soccer with that kid out in the street. And now, his rifle was trained on the boy's heart. He'd seen the threat under the boy's clothing, but the tear in his eye made Sean pause his trigger finger. That single second cost more than Sean had in his account. It robbed Sean of his faith in humanity.

They caught the father within days. The man was tried and convicted. As he was led away, he went proclaiming his pride in his son for the sacrifice he'd made for the cause.

That turned Sean's stomach every time he thought about it. Whatever it was called, that wasn't love. It was cowardice and perversion. No god would ever have a father murder a son in his name.

The tendrils of the nightmare slowly loosened their grip on him. But he still wanted to lash out. His hand itched for a rifle to hug close. He wanted to push away anyone who got near him.

Even as dark and gruesome as the nightmare was, Sean kept his eyes closed. He was not ready to face this day. But the sun had other ideas. And so he opened his eyes.

Sean's whole body felt as though he'd been cast into the fire and pulled out. His skin felt brittle and tight. It hurt to move his limbs. Still, he preferred the dream to his current reality.

Ruhi was pregnant.

The possibility of being with Ruhi, in reality, had always been a dream. A dream he could only access during his waking hours. Those dreams never came true.

He knew that Dr. Pasteurizer, or whatever his name was, was all wrong for her. Sean had been certain she'd break up with him sooner or later. He was glad that it had come sooner. But the guy had gone and broken up with her after he'd gotten her pregnant.

Just as Sean couldn't fathom turning a child into a weapon of war, he couldn't understand a father who would abandon a child.

In the modern world, there were far too many single moms for his comfort. Too many women that had the title shoved on them, not by their own choice. Sean wanted to find Ruhi's ex and put his fist down his throat.

But it wasn't his place. Ruhi was his nurse. He had no business interfering in her personal life.

However, holding her in his arms had been the first time in a long time that he didn't feel the constant heat at his back. As she'd settled her head against his shoulder, the constant screaming in his head had stopped. As he'd run the cool cloth over her face, he'd only smelled the fresh floral scent of her skin lotion.

It had been the only peace he'd had in a year. He

wished he could have more of it. But he knew better. Love was not in his cards, not with a scar on his face and inside his soul.

Sean dressed and headed out to greet the day. He wasn't the only one up. The soldiers of the ranch were used to early mornings as part of their duties. It was another reason ranch life suited them so well.

Sean fell into work beside his squad. The men had been proud of their work as they'd built the school. The loss of the building had been a blow to their spirits as much as the explosion had taken a pound of flesh out of each of them.

But this ranch had given them all back their purpose. Working with the therapy horses, tending to the farm animals, tilling the soil, watching things grow and prosper under their care, all of this work had brought each man back from the horrors of war.

"The school called and told me that kid, James, the one with bronchitis, he stayed home from school today," said Dylan. He held the wood of a broken fence as Sean pounded in a post.

"Do you think we should stop by and check on him?" asked Fran. He hefted the other end of the new railing.

Dylan shrugged as he fit the wood into place.

"She said he misses a lot of days from school, but his grades are always great."

"Do you think we should talk to his parents?" asked Fran.

"I gave the counselor the number to the ranch."

Sean stayed mute during the conversation. He supported the youth program, but he wanted no active part in it. Yesterday was his one and only starring role.

The sun rose higher in the sky. The rays licked a trail up Sean's back. Sean took a deep breath, trying to shove the memories of war away. But the sun's rays were relentless under the Montana sky.

"Jeffries," said Dylan. "Don't you have an appointment with Dr. Patel today?"

He didn't. But Sean got Dylan's meaning. The other soldiers never spoke of his PTSD. They didn't really speak of their own, except with Dr. Patel. Each man knew the warning signs. And Sean was clearly displaying them now under the heat of the sun. Without another word, Sean handed the hammer over to Fran and took off toward the medical suite.

When he arrived at the doctor's office, Dr. Patel's door was closed. The walk and the cool air had done him good. Sean's thoughts were his own again. And his only thought was of Ruhi.

He made his way down the hall and to her office. But when he got there, he saw that her door was also closed. The lights were off, and the room vacant.

That was odd. Sean knew her schedule. It was her day at the ranch.

"She's taking the day off." Dr. Patel came up behind Sean. His steps were slow; his hands were visible. The psychologist knew better than to sneak up on a soldier, especially a trained sniper. "I didn't realize you had an appointment with her today."

"I don't. I was just ... I had a question and ..."

Dr. Patel eyed him with that patient smile. Sean didn't talk much in his sessions with the psychologist. And still, the man was able to tell exactly what he was thinking.

"There was a sick kid yesterday," said Sean. "And she helped him. I just had a question about his treatment."

Dr. Patel nodded. "Ruhi said that her stomach disagreed with her."

This was one of those times Sean was happy he had a limited range of facial expressions. He didn't smile or frown or nod. He kept his face perfectly immobile.

"But I think it might be personal troubles."

Again, Sean held his tongue and his facial muscles still.

"It's hard being a father in these days, especially with girls pushing for the equality of the sexes. I think it confuses men because there are some things that men should do for their wives and their families. But my Ruhi, she thinks she's supposed to do it all by herself."

Sean sure hoped she wasn't trying to raise this child all by herself. But he also hoped that the baby daddy would stay out of the picture.

"Listen to me," chuckled Dr. Patel. "I've turned into a psychologist who tells my woes to a patient. But you have that kind of face." Dr. Patel winked.

Sean managed the smallest of smiles. Only Ruhi and her father could get him to lower his guard enough to stretch his facial muscles.

No. That wasn't true. The guys could in rare moments. And Maggie was always saying something that made him shake his head if not crack a smile. And Eva always invaded his space with her maternal hugs. And he found he liked watching *Dr. Who* episodes with Sarai.

Sean was going to miss the women of the ranch when he had to move. He would be smiling a lot less when he was gone. There would hardly be any women in his life that he would feel comfortable sitting next to or hugging. A woman whose hair he didn't mind holding back as she let the contents of her stomach wash down a sink. A woman who he'd love to sit in silence with on the cold tile floor.

"I was going to take Ruhi some Mulligatawny soup after work, but I have to run to the church which is on the other side of town."

"I can take it."

"You sure it's no trouble?"

"None at all."

Sean followed Dr. Patel back down the hall to his office. The doctor handed him the Tupperware. It was warm in his hands, and he welcomed the heat.

CHAPTER SIX

The white stick fell to the linoleum floor with a clatter. Ruhi was surprised it didn't shatter into a million pieces because that's how she felt. Her life, her plans, her future, were now all scattered in pieces by something so small as a little white stick.

There were no lines to count on the stick. No pink or blue colors. This test was digital. It told her in black and white.

She was pregnant.

It had told her twice. She'd brought a two-pack just to be sure. The first one had said the same thing. There was no such thing as a false positive when it came to pregnancy. If the hormones were there, then a baby was in the oven.

Ruhi's hands went to her abdomen. There was something living in there, someone. A little person that she was now responsible for. They'd been there for some time now, likely a few weeks, and she hadn't known about them.

Oh, no! She'd had at least three bottles of wine over the last month. And she'd gone out dancing in a smoky club at least four times. And there was that tuna salad the other day. Wasn't tuna bad for babies?

Great. She was already off to a great start as Mother of the Year. She had neglected her child for weeks, exposing him or her to all the wrong elements. And to top that off, they wouldn't get a dad as part of the deal.

Ruhi looked up on her mantle. There was a picture of her standing between both her parents on her graduation day. She knew that each of her siblings had a similar picture. Her parents had given each of their children the same amount of love, or more, when it came time that they needed the extra attention.

Ruhi had never once felt neglected or alone, even when she wanted to be by herself. She'd known her whole life that her family, especially her parents, would be there for her before she knew she needed them.

Her child wouldn't know the same. Unless ...

She looked down at her cell phone. Maybe she should give Michael a chance to be a dad? It wasn't exactly an option. He was the father. He could choose to not be in their child's life, but that wouldn't change the fact that he was the child's father.

It wasn't as though she were trying to get back together with him. He'd made it clear there was no spark. The problem was there had been a spark, and it was growing in her belly.

Ruhi picked up her phone. Her stomach rumbled, but nothing came up. She just had a sick feeling that settled there.

Michael was still in her number six spot, after her parents and siblings. She hit the little heart next to his name and listened while the phone rang. And rang.

Finally, it clicked over and Ruhi nearly threw up.

"Hello?" said a feminine voice. The voice was sleep riddled.

Had he already moved on? It had barely been two days. And his new chick was answering his phone. She'd never pulled that while they were together.

Ruhi quickly disconnected the line. Humiliation

filled her gut but unlike anything else she tried to keep from coming up, it stayed down in there.

A knock at her door had her jerking to attention. It was probably her father. She'd called in sick that morning. He or her mother was sure to be by with some spicy soup to cure her.

But she didn't have a case of a common cold. She had a case of the stupids. The only known cure was not repeating past mistakes.

Ruhi tossed her phone to the side. Then she picked it back up and deleted Michael's number. Not only from her favorites, but from her contacts.

Ruhi went to the door. She opened without asking who it was. It didn't matter if it was her mother or father, she'd have to tell them sooner or later that she was pregnant out of wedlock and would be raising the child on her own.

Her hand halted on the doorknob. She turned back to the picture over the mantle. They were smiling proudly at her there. The next picture wouldn't be filled with pride. There would be a look of disappointment on their faces when she told them her newest accomplishment. It wouldn't be the first time.

They'd tried setting her up for years for an arranged marriage with a parade of nice Indian men that they'd vetted thoroughly. It wasn't that Ruhi was determined to marry outside her race. She just was suspicious of any Indian boy that showed her interest, certain they were a plant by someone in her family.

Eventually, her family took the hint and left her to her own devices in her dating life. But she didn't miss their telling glances that said though they supported her, they disagreed with her track.

Dating wasn't the only track they disagreed with her on. They didn't understand why she stopped at Nurse Practitioner and didn't get her Doctorate degree.

They didn't always see eye to eye with her recycling, environmentalist, and health choices. But they indulged her.

Could they indulge her being a single, unwed, career mom?

She knew they would. But there would be that period of disappointment at the edge of their smiles, in the corner of their eyes.

Maybe she should call Michael back? If she showed up with a husband they'd be less disappointed. But no. She had her pride. If he'd moved on, then she would too.

Besides, she was swearing off men for the

foreseeable future. That was a guarantee now that she'd have a child in tow. Kids were known to put dampers on a woman's social life.

Ruhi took a deep breath and pulled open the door. "What are you doing here?"

Standing on her stoop, in the dim light of the hallway was Sean Jeffries. He held up a covered soup bowl she recognized as her mother's. "Your father sent me with soup."

Ruhi sighed. She wasn't sure if it was because of the soup or because she had a reprieve for a little while longer before she told her parents about her predicament. A predicament that only she and Sean knew about.

"How are you feeling?" he asked.

Ruhi waved him in. "I haven't thrown up today. But my stomach isn't sure about spicy foods."

"I also brought crackers and a banana. I hear that's good for ... you know."

"You can say it, Sean. I'm pregnant." Ruhi tugged open the container filled with her mother's spicy soup that would always warm her heart when she was under the weather. The moment the curry hit her nose, she slammed the lid shut so that the smell couldn't travel any further into her queasy body.

Sean seated himself in the center of her small

love seat and watched her beneath his hooded gaze. He made certain to turn the right side of his face away from her. Ruhi walked over to the right side of him and sat. The warmth coming off his body reminded her of being tucked in on a winter's night by her mother, of sipping chai tea with her father on Sunday afternoons.

Before she knew it, she'd tucked her legs underneath herself and settled into the nook of Sean's shoulder. She was too tired and too comfortable to feel any shame about leaning on him. Though she was certain this wasn't the most professional of moves, Sean was the only person in her corner right now.

And besides, he wasn't complaining. He sat beside her, his arm wrapped across the back of the sofa. He'd always been the perfect gentleman. All of the soldiers on the ranch had been since the moment she turned up to help with their healing. Not one had made a move on her, not even Xavier who was a notorious skirt chaser. It was likely out of respect for her father. But more likely it was how these veterans were built, to protect and to serve.

Or was that police officers? Ruhi couldn't be bothered. The warm comfort and cozy silence were all she cared to focus on.

"Have you told ... him?"

Ruhi shook her head. When she did, her nose brushed against Sean's shoulder. He smelled of wood and outdoors and a hint of the spices from her mom's soup. For some reason, the smell of the spices on him didn't bother her stomach one ounce.

Ruhi lifted her gaze. Her eyes glanced over Sean's scar. When she'd first seen the deep grooves, she'd thought they made him look angry. But she'd never once in an entire year heard Sean raise his voice. She couldn't remember a time when he'd looked directly at her for more than the second it took to answer her litany of health questions.

He gazed down at her now, and she saw that he had golden flecks in his hazel eyes. The cruel scar highlighted the gracious curve of his upper lip. She'd touched the scar numerous times and knew it to be stiff and unyielding. She'd never touched his lips. She'd bet they were soft as velvet.

Ruhi sat up straight. The motion made her nauseous. Sean's hand at her back instantly quelled the sick feeling.

"Michael was otherwise engaged with someone else when I called. He's the one that ended our relationship. He's already moved onto someone new."

Sean shook his head, anger clear on the grooved lines of his face. "I'm not his biggest fan. Still, the child deserves a father."

Ruhi wrapped her arms around herself. "I just wish the father were someone else."

Sean's arms came around her. She didn't brush him away. She hadn't realized she was so starved for affection. When was the last time Michael had simply held her?

"What if it was?" Sean's words were spoken so quietly she thought she'd imagined he'd said anything at all.

"What if what was?"

He turned to her. His gaze wide enough for her to see his hazel flecks. He tugged at his chin before he spoke again. "What if the father were someone else."

"What do you mean?" she asked.

"What if it were me?"

Now not only her stomach was playing tricks on her, but Ruhi was also hearing things. "I'm sorry, what?"

Now, Sean avoided eye contact. "It just seems that we might be able to help each other out. I need a wife to stay on the ranch. You need a father for your child."

She stared at him. Because of his scar, Sean couldn't make the normal range of facial expressions. He always looked serious, some would even say angry. But Ruhi could always tell what was on his mind by what she saw in his eyes.

Slowly his gaze slid to her, and she saw that he was completely serious.

CHAPTER SEVEN

It was too late to take them back. Sean's words were already out of his mouth and in her ears. And, oh boy, had she heard them.

Ruhi stared at him. Her lips parted, her eyes wide. Her hand was on her abdomen, as though she were protecting her baby from the ludicrous idea.

Sean had no idea what had gotten into him.

Wait. Yes, he did. It was the feel of her resting against his shoulder. It was the vulnerable, lost look in her eyes as she'd gazed up at him.

It had all felt so right. And if she married him, even in name only, she could feel free to do that every day.

She could come home from a long day at the office taking care of others, and he would take care of her. He would bring her comfort foods to nourish her. He would listen to her as she told him all of her secrets and worries. He would hold her as she rested and take on any load that she bore, including the one she carried in her belly.

But it was a pipe dream; a self-destructive mission. Instead of a vest containing an explosive, Sean had opened his heart. His misguided efforts had just blown up in his face.

Ruhi was turning the proposal over in her head as she stared at him. She obviously thought it was the most ridiculous idea ever. He should've delivered the soup and turned to go without breaching her threshold.

"I'm sorry," he said rising from the couch. "It was a stupid idea. I was just trying to help."

He took a few steps to the door. She didn't stop him. She didn't move. She was still frozen in the same position that he'd left her on the small love seat.

Had the idea of being with him disgusted her so much? Now she wouldn't be comfortable treating him. He'd ruined everything, and she wouldn't want to see him professionally anymore.

"I just want to be sure you understood I wasn't

suggesting we behave like a real married couple," he said. "It would be platonic. Would've been, I mean."

Why was he still talking? He couldn't remember the last time he'd talked this much. For the last year, he had been a man of few words to even those who were closest to him.

One reason was because every time he opened his mouth, he felt the traction of the scarred skin on his cheek. And so he kept quiet and let the scab lie. Now he barely felt the scar, and he couldn't seem to keep his mouth closed.

"You wouldn't have to be a single mother. You'd have a partner. I could stay on the ranch. We could raise the child there around a huge family who would have each other's back. But it was a ridiculous idea."

"That doesn't sound ridiculous at all." Her voice was so quiet he nearly hadn't heard her. Slowly she turned to him. Her gaze lifted and so did the hope in his heart. "Platonic?"

"I beg your pardon?" Sean took a step toward her. It was a careful step, as though he were making his way through a live minefield.

Ruhi stood. Her steps were just as cautious as his. "Our relationship? We'd be platonic? Equals?

Sharing all the duties of the household, finances, and parenthood?"

Now Sean's jaw decided to clench. He swallowed, trying to get moisture to the inside of his mouth. When he was able to open his jaw he swore he heard the creak of hinges. "Of course."

"What if you wanted to date?" she asked.

A harsh breath left his nose as he laughed. Date? He hadn't thought of dating anyone but her in a year. But he didn't dare tell her that. His heart had already been put through enough tonight.

"I'm not looking to date anyone," he said. "Not looking like this." His hand lifted and motioned to the side of his face.

Ruhi followed the direction of his fingers. She cocked her head and frowned. Sean hadn't felt self-conscious when she looked at him since the first time she'd rested her fingers on his chin and lifted his gaze to meet hers. Now, all his insecurities rushed in. Consciously, he angled the right side of his body away from her. But her next words had him dropping his guard entirely.

"You don't realize how handsome you are," she said. "That the goodness in you shines through."

No. No, he did not realize that. He did not believe that. "I'm not a good man."

"I don't believe that. Not for one second." She took a step toward him. More sure and less cautious this time.

Sean took a step back. "I've done … things, Ruhi."

She nodded. She knew about his PTSD. It was part of his medical chart. Though they'd never talked about it before. She likely knew where much of his stress stemmed from. Still, she took another step toward him.

"You protected people," she said. "The innocent civilians in other countries, and all of the people in your country."

She stopped moving when she was standing before him. She took a deep inhale. Her hand came to rest on her belly.

Sean held his breath. He didn't breathe again until she exhaled.

She looked at him. Her eyes filled with so much vulnerability that he took another step toward her. But her outburst of laughter halted him. For the second time tonight, Sean felt as though his heart had been blown to bits.

"This is crazy," she said. "I can't do this to you. I can't ruin your life just because I screwed up mine."

She thought marriage to him would ruin his life? Not hers? For the second time tonight, his heart sewed itself back up and reached toward hope again.

"You wouldn't be ruining my life," Sean said. "You helped to heal me. You are the reason I can get up in the morning and face the day looking like this."

She opened her mouth to protest, but Sean held up his hand. This confession was the closest he'd ever get to telling her his true feelings.

"I've never told you how much what you do for me means to me. If this is how I can show my appreciation, by coming to your rescue in your time of need, I would be honored to be your hero."

The moment was ripe for him to get down on his knee and propose. But he knew better. He knew that wouldn't impress Ruhi. And so, instead, he offered her his hand.

"Ruhi Patel, I would be honored to be your partner in raising this child. Please consider taking my hand and being my partner in life."

For the first time in days, Ruhi woke without immediately rushing to bend over the toilet. Her stomach grumbled with hunger instead of upset. She felt light instead of foggy.

Her hand rubbed over her abdomen. Her belly was still flat, but she felt different. She had the knowledge that a new life was within her. And she, herself, was starting a new life.

She was getting married. Or at least she thought she was getting married. She hadn't given Sean a final answer. She'd told him she'd think about his proposal.

Lying in bed after he'd left, she'd thought of nothing else. It would solve so many problems. The first being her desire not to raise a child alone. Then there was the waiting disappointment that would dawn on her parent's face when they learned her news. But with Sean by her side, they wouldn't frown.

Her parents loved each of the soldiers. Anyone of them would've been on their husband-approved list for their single, professional daughter. That included Sean; the gentle soul whose gaze was haunted by the ravages of war.

Sean didn't attend church services, but Ruhi had seen him more times than she could count out in the field with a Bible in his hand. Her father had mentioned that they had prayed together in a few of his sessions. Sean preferred his fellowship in private.

He was a practical man, not given to romantic overtures. His marriage proposal hadn't been poetic. It had been practical and well thought out. She hadn't been swept off her feet. But she had found it thought-provoking.

It made sense. She couldn't think of a single reason she shouldn't consider Sean's proposal seriously. Love obviously wasn't coming her way in this lifetime. She'd dated enough to know that the spark would likely never ignite in her heart. It was high time she stopped looking for it.

She now had another life to care for besides her

own. She had to start thinking practically. But could she spend the rest of her life with Sean in a platonic relationship? Could he? Could a man be platonic?

Ruhi wasn't so sure it was biologically possible. She'd never seen Sean with a woman the entire year he'd been on the ranch. He rarely left the grounds. He rarely lifted his gaze to any of the women who worked on the ranch. Except for the other wives, and her.

She and Sean got along fine. He was a decent man, loyal and kind. He was even funny every once in a while. He respected what she did and trusted her judgment. They both were financially stable.

Heck, she'd been having the best relationship of her life and hadn't even known it.

The only problem was that there wasn't any love between them. But was that really a problem? If love hadn't found her in all these years, it probably wasn't paying her any mind. Not everyone married for love. The vast amount of pairings were business arrangements, and they worked. Why not hers?

And in a few years, if Sean wanted a divorce because he found someone who'd love him, someone whom he loved in return, then she'd honor that and let him out of the marriage. It was just a contract, after all. There would be no need to hold him to it if the arrangement no longer served him.

With that thought in mind, Ruhi dressed and headed in to work. She wasn't due at the ranch until later in the afternoon. She did her rounds at the free clinic quickly. Even though the clinic urged twenty minute max visits, quickly and free often clashed.

There was a mom of five and each of the children had pink eye. A sixteen-year-old boy came in with what Ruhi confirmed to be an STD. A fourteen-year-old came in and was diagnosed with the flu instead of the pregnancy she suspected. She couldn't turn any of these people away with a doctor's note and a thank you for your patronage. Each deserved her undivided attention and a heartfelt talk.

So Ruhi didn't walk out of the clinic until well after lunch. When she pulled up to the Purple Heart Ranch she saw the bright yellow school bus carrying the boys of the youth program pulling in as well. The last kid straggling off the bus was coughing.

Ruhi recognized him as the kid she'd diagnosed with bronchitis. James, he'd said his name was. Ruhi made her way over to the kid before he headed into the fields with the others.

"Hey, James," she called out. "Feeling any better?"

The kid looked around as though he wasn't sure she was talking to him. "Oh. Hi. Yeah. I'm fine."

Ruhi had been saying the same thing for a couple of days, and she wasn't. Not until just this morning when she felt she'd worked out a new five-year plan. One that included a marriage of convenience, a hunt for the best preschools, and perhaps her own practice. Montana was one of the few states that allowed a nurse practitioner to practice on her own. Then she could spend as much time as needed with her patients to treat their ailments from the inside and the outside.

"Were you able to get that medicine I prescribed?" she asked the kid.

"Oh, my dad said he'll get it today."

The shiftiness of the kid gave Ruhi pause. Clearly, he wasn't telling the truth. Hadn't it already been two days since she'd seen him? If left untreated, bronchitis could develop into something worse.

"I may have some cough syrup in my office. Why don't you come and get it?"

But he was already shaking his head and backing

away. "I gotta go catch up with everybody else. I already missed a day. But I'll come before I go."

"Okay." She could do nothing but watch the kid go. For the moment. She'd give the school nurse a call when she got to her office and see if there was anything that could be done on their end.

"We're having trouble with that one." Dylan parted from the shadows and came to stand beside her. "He's a loner. Doesn't like anyone seeing him as weak."

"Yeah, I know the type," Ruhi said. "Hey, have you seen Sean?"

"He was in the stalls. He drove over to your place yesterday?" There was a lift to Dylan's eye.

That was the only thing she wasn't looking forward to about living on a ranch. There was very little privacy, even when your doors were shut. But just the same as everyone put their nose in everyone else's business, loyalty and devotion ran deep. Ranch families were real families.

Still, Ruhi wasn't ready to have her business divulged just yet. She shrugged, evading Dylan's prying blue gaze. "I wasn't feeling well. He brought me some soup. I just wanted to thank him."

"Hmm."

Ruhi ignored the loaded sound that Dylan made

and headed to the stalls. She found Sean inside mucking out one of the stalls. She called his name, but he didn't respond. She could see the wires of earbuds hanging from his ears. Shouting would do no good, so she went up and tapped him on the back.

Sean spun around, rake held high like a bat. Ruhi instantly raised her arms to cover her face. Through her fingers, she saw Sean's eyes go wide.

He dropped the rake and doubled over as though he were going to be sick. "Oh, my God. Oh, my God."

Ruhi straightened and went to him. She reached out her hand and then withdrew it at the last minute. "Sean?"

His eyes were closed tight. His hands balled into fists. "You can't sneak up on me like that." His voice was so quiet, so broken.

Ruhi had never had the occasion to seek him out. He was always waiting for her at her office door. "I'm sorry. I'll know better next time."

"Next time?"

The tremor in his voice shook something deep inside her. Ruhi didn't like to see people in pain, especially not those she cared about. Sean had been there in her time of need, and now, somehow, she'd hurt him.

Sean looked from her eyes, then to her belly. "No. There can't be a next time. What was I thinking? I could hurt you or the baby."

"You would never ..."

"Not on purpose, no. But what if I get surprised or startled. What if the baby wanders in my room at night and I'm having a nightmare and ..."

"Sean, I know you. I trust you. You would never hurt anyone."

"I have hurt people."

"In the service."

He stared at her. There was so much vulnerability in his gaze. She wanted to wrap him up and protect him. Instead, she turned away and looked out the door at the midday sun.

Was she making the right decision? She'd never come face to face with Sean's demons. That look in his eyes, however brief, when he didn't recognize her, that had scared her. Was she making a mistake putting her child under the same roof with this man?

She turned back to him just as he was taking a step to her. Somehow they collided. As she teetered toward the ground Sean rotated his body so that he landed on the hard ground with her on top of him.

That cinched the deal for Ruhi. Despite what he

may think, Ruhi had no doubt that Sean would do whatever was necessary to make sure she and her baby were taken care of and out of harm's way.

With his hard body under hers, she also began wondering how long the platonic part of their plan would last. By the way he gazed at her lips she wondered if he were thinking the same thing. Again the thought raced through her mind; maybe this was a mistake. But for a different reason.

"Ruhi?" her father called out. "Dylan told me you were in here. I have a surprise for you."

Her father pulled the doors to the stables open, letting in the full light of the day. The surprise was that her mother was with him. Her parents looked down at Ruhi who lay on top of Sean.

No one moved. Not her parents framed in the doorway. Not Ruhi or Sean tangled on the ground. The silence in the barn was deafening.

"It's okay," Ruhi said. "We're getting married."

CHAPTER NINE

Sean had been caught by parents before with girls. It had never been more than kissing. The parents had never been too upset when they found their daughters in his embrace. Sean was a great student, came from a great family, and had a great future ahead of him.

That was then.

This was now.

Dr. Patel steepled his fingers on his large desk. They didn't sit in the arranged chair and chaise lounge like when Sean was at his therapy sessions. This wasn't a session. This was an interrogation.

"So," began the doctor. "You and Ruhi?"

That was it? That's how Dr. Patel planned to start

this conversation. Where was Sean supposed to take that? There were so many directions.

So, he and Ruhi were caught in a compromising position.

So, he and Ruhi were a thing.

So, he and Ruhi should consider entering a pie eating competition.

"It wasn't what you think?" That seemed a safe bet.

Dr. Patel waited patiently for Sean to tell him what to think. What did Sean want the father of the woman he was secretly in love with and was about to enter into a marriage of convenience with, to be the beard for her deadbeat baby daddy ex-boyfriend to think? Anything out of his mouth would be a lie.

"I care very deeply for your daughter."

That was the truth. Sean wouldn't sully his relationship with this man who had helped him with anything but the truth.

"I know," said Dr. Patel.

Of course, he knew. Dr. Patel knew everything. Sean and the others long since held the belief that the man had a direct line to God. Sean was certain the two chatted about the inner workings of everyone's lives and God sent Dr. Patel to do his good work on earth while He remained in heaven.

"And that's what worries me," Dr. Patel continued. "My daughter has very non-traditional ideas of relationships. I know you come from a traditional family. I know, despite what you may think of yourself, that you want a wife and children for yourself. I'm not sure that Ruhi will ever want those things for herself."

Wow. For the first time likely in his entire life, Dr. Patel got it wrong.

Sean did want those things. He wanted a family of his own. He wanted a wife to come home to every night. He wanted children to toss into the air and teach life lessons to. The problem was the only woman he saw himself having any of those things with was Ruhi.

"Being a father is the hardest job," Dr. Patel continued. "I thought being married was hard work, but a husband and wife always work toward a compromise. A father and his children, that's a different relationship. You can guide them, but inevitably you have to let them go off and make their own decisions. It's hardest when you know the path they're on is not the best."

Sean knew that. His own family, who he loved dearly, urged him to come home after he was discharged from the service. But Sean knew that being back in civilian life, even surrounded by the people who loved him most, wouldn't help in his healing. He knew he needed his fellow soldiers around him, men who would understand and not be offended when he needed to go quiet and be alone.

"I would be thrilled if my daughter married someone like you. I would be over the moon if it was, in fact, you that she chose. Freud would say she's rebelling against her parental ideal. But I don't think she's happy. I know she's not happy. I worry for her, but I have to let her walk this path and hope that she ends up in the place she's meant to be. The problem is, Sean, I don't want you getting hurt along the way."

Sean couldn't help but crack a smile even though it hurt his face. This man would be his father in law. He couldn't ask for a better role model, a more solid patriarch than the father he already had. But Dr. Patel could easily stand next to his old man.

Sean scooted the chair away from the desk. He ran his hands over his jeans to smooth the fabric as he stood. "Dr. Patel, I have something very important to ask you. I would like to ask you for your daughter's hand in marriage."

Dr. Patel frowned. "Haven't you been listening, son?"

Son. Sean liked the sound of that. "I have. I've already asked Ruhi to be my wife, and she's said yes."

Sean had never seen Dr. Patel at a loss for words.

"I would've asked you first but it all happened so fast."

"Forgive me, but why? I know she cares for you, but not in a romantic way. Meanwhile, I've seen the way you look at her. That is most definitely in a romantic way."

Sean rubbed at his chin. Dr. Patel was right. Sean was in love, while Ruhi was only in trouble.

"Does this have to do with the zoning?"

Sean sat back down. He nodded as he did so.

"I can't say I'm not surprised that she would help in that matter. I assume you two have some kind of short-term agreement in place?"

They'd never discussed a duration to the arrangement. Sean wanted it to last a lifetime, even if it remained platonic. Just being near Ruhi made him feel alive.

"But you have real feelings for her?"

"I do," Sean admitted.

"Does she know that?"

"I don't think so." He couldn't tell Ruhi's father

that their marriage would be platonic. Especially not with a baby already growing inside her.

"What about... what was his name?"

That said something if the girlfriend's father couldn't remember the boyfriend's name. "Michael. He's leaving for a job overseas."

"Oh." Dr. Patel didn't look put out over that. "I'm worried about this arrangement, but I'm also pleased. I meant it when I said I can't think of a better man for her."

"You're not worried about my ... episodes?"

Dr. Patel took a deep breath. "There are some protocols we can put in place for your nightmares. But I trust you."

Ruhi had said the same thing. Sean would do everything in his power to keep their trust even in this relationship that had its roots in a lie.

CHAPTER TEN

"I thought you were dating Mitchel?"

Ruhi looked over at her mother as she mispronounced her ex's name. Deeksha Patel was dressed in colorful pants and a bright shirt. You could take the girl out of New Delhi, but you can't take New Dehli out of the girl.

"His name was Michael," said Ruhi. "And we broke up."

Why could no one remember his name? They'd dated for five months. Okay, they'd been casually seeing each other for four months. But she'd introduced Michael to her family and friends. Hardly anyone could remember his name. True, Ruhi wanted everyone to forget they ever knew him now.

"So you and Sean are casual?" Her mom grimaced when she said the word. There was the disappointment at the crinkle of her eyes.

"Sean and I are … a bit more than casual."

And there it was. Her mother's eyes lit up. Ruhi tried not to let that light get to her, but she couldn't help it. She loved being in the light of her parents' praise. It had been a long time since that had happened.

She'd gotten great grades in school. She'd done well in sports. But all of her accomplishments were largely over. She'd hoped getting the Doctors Without Borders position would gain her another bout of praise, but that career opportunity had been stolen out from under her by that Mitchel-guy.

Ruhi knew this pregnancy would get a crinkle of disappointment when her parents learned it was another man's child. A man whose name they couldn't even bother to remember. But with her pact with Sean did they ever need to find out?

There was also her impending marriage to Sean. She knew her family wanted to see her settled. Despite how much her parents pushed her and her siblings to advance in academics and their chosen profession, Ruhi knew they both believed that marriage and family were life's ultimate goals.

"I told you," said Ruhi. "We're getting married."

"So, that wasn't a joke back there in the barn?"

"No, Mommy. I was completely serious." She was also whining like a child whose parents thought she was fibbing. "He asked, and I said yes."

The air gushed from her mother. Her mother's arms flew around her. She squeezed Ruhi so tight Ruhi thought she might burst.

A girlish giggle escaped her mother as she released Ruhi from her hold. "We'll get on wedding planning straight away and ..."

Oh, no. The pride of marriage and being in a union Ruhi could take. But a traditional Indian wedding that lasted days? No. There she was putting her foot down.

"We're just going to go to City Hall, Mommy."

The pride and joy and giggles came to a scratching halt, like a needle careening off a record. In an instant, her mother's joy of her announcement was washed away. Deeksha Patel took a deep breath to begin what Ruhi knew would be a long diatribe that would only end when Ruhi gave in.

"You are my last child."

"I know, Mommy, but you got to do this two other times already."

"Don't you want to celebrate your union to Sean?"

"It's not about the celebration, Mommy. It's about the vows we make to each other. The commitment. That's what I want to focus on."

Where did that come from? It wasn't as though Ruhi had never planned to get married. She didn't ever see herself having a huge wedding. She didn't like being the center of attention. She just liked having her family's praise. That was all she needed, her family around her as she went through this.

And Sean.

Sean had been her rock over these last couple of days. He'd infiltrated all of her plans for the future. How had he become so integral to her life?

What she did know was that she couldn't do this without him. She didn't want to. And she also didn't want to make a big fuss over the start of their union. She knew he wouldn't want that as well. Just like her, Sean didn't like the spotlight.

"Sean and I are both private people. We don't like to have a spectacle around us."

"Oh," said her mother. She rubbed at her cheek, the right side of her cheek. "I see. He's worried people will stare. But he's so handsome."

Sean was handsome. The scar added to that. It

gave him an air of mystery. Ruhi watched some of the other women working on the ranch give him a few lingering glances. Sean never noticed, of course. He was always too busy looking down and hiding his face.

But not with her. He looked at her. Mainly because she forced him to when she was treating him. But he also gave her his smiles, which she knew was hard for him because it was an uncomfortable gesture.

"Ruhi?"

Ruhi blinked as her mother called her name. She'd been lost thinking about Sean's smiles. She quickly brushed those thoughts off. That was not a path she was going down.

Sean might keep giving her smiles, she was sure he would. But they would always be friendly. She couldn't handle anything more than that. There'd been too much rejection in her life. She just needed to focus on her baby. And her plan.

"Don't worry," said her mother. "I'll plan everything. You'll have the wedding here, like the other soldiers. And we'll only invite a few family members."

Ruhi inhaled, ready to put up a fight. But as the air traveled down her lungs, she realized that she was tired. There was no fight left in her today. "Of course, Mommy."

Her mother's eyes lit up. She wrapped her arms around her daughter. Ruhi heard no more of her mother's planning, which quickly went beyond the small affair she'd just promised. Ruhi just nodded and went along and let her mother take care of everything.

CHAPTER ELEVEN

The colors were so bright that Sean had to shade his eyes. Mrs. Patel said she invited a few people, just close family, and friends. All the seats were taken at the gazebo and a crowd stood for rows behind them. All in vibrant colors.

He'd been told this was the small family ceremony known as the *ganesh pooja*. This intimate ceremony happened on the first night of a traditional Indian wedding. A typical wedding, he'd learned, lasted three days.

Ruhi had lost many of the battles over the planning of their wedding. The only two she'd won were having the wedding on Saturday of this week, and she had insisted that they condense everything into one day. Mrs. Patel had grumbled but assented.

Sean assumed Ruhi hadn't gotten a look at the latest guest list.

They'd both wanted something small. But their parents had other ideas for their children.

Mixed in with the bright sari's, Sean saw his parents and their friends. The men were in suits and the women wore their best church hats, Sunday crowns, and lacy fascinators. The two families were mingling in what was called the *sangeet*, which usually happened the second evening of the traditional Indian wedding.

Sean admittedly was feeling overwhelmed. It had been a while since he'd been around that many people and that much noise. He focused on his breathing and the sound of his heartbeat.

"Sean?"

Dylan made sure to announce himself before placing a hand on Sean's back. Sean still tensed. Not from his friend's gesture. Sean tensed because he'd been found in his hiding place.

"How are you holding up?" Dylan asked looking out at the gathered crowd. "It's not exactly a small affair."

Mixed in with his and Ruhi's families and friends, Sean saw his ranch family. Reed was introducing Sarai to Sean's parents. Sean saw

Xavier chatting with his older sister—he'd have to go put a kibosh on that. But Fran was already stepping in between the two and introducing Sean's sister to his wife. Maggie was making the rounds amongst the Patel side of the family with her dogs in tow.

"You ready for this?" Dylan asked.

Sean wasn't sure if his friend was asking about the marriage, or the wedding, or his future? He was trying to concentrate on Dylan's words and not the cacophony of sounds. He was trying to stay in the shade so the sun wouldn't beat down on him and remind him of the feel of the fire. He was trying to pick out the familiar faces and not be on the constant lookout for a threat.

Looking out, even though Sean didn't recognize some of the faces, he knew there was no threat there. Everyone's faces were filled with joy and anticipation. And it was all in support of his union to Ruhi.

These were all family and friends. No one was there to hurt anyone. Everyone was there to celebrate. Still, his heartbeat refused to settle.

"We've got your back," Dylan said. "You know that."

Sean nodded. "I know that."

"Say the word and we can make the ceremony private."

Sean shook his head. Mrs. Patel and his mother had gone to so much trouble to make this ceremony happen in just a matter of days. He was getting what he wanted, the woman of his dreams' hand in marriage. He could give their families what they wanted, a big gathering to celebrate. He could do this.

"I just need a minute alone."

Dylan nodded and stepped out of Sean's way. The moment his friend was out of sight, Sean slunk around the corner. He made his way back toward the living quarters. He was unconsciously headed towards Ruhi.

He knew he'd found her when he heard a lot of feminine giggling. They were in Maggie and Dylan's house, the largest on the lot. Ruhi had been by his place— their place—to drop off her things, but she hadn't yet spent the night in their home.

Sean knocked at the screen door. "It's me. Sean. Can I have a word with Ruhi?"

"You can't see her before the wedding," Mrs. Patel called out. "It's bad luck."

"I know. I just want to talk to her for a minute. Alone if possible."

The women came to the front door. Mrs. Patel looked up at him with a pinched expression, that instantly softened. She lifted up on her tiptoes and planted a kiss on the left side of his face. It was a move that only Ruhi had attempted, but Sean held still for Mrs. Patel. It was uncomfortable, but he allowed it.

"Don't you dare turn around," warned Mrs. Patel.

Sean stood in the doorway with his back to his bride as the women walked out of the house and onto the porch. Sean's gaze focused on the gathered crowd. He couldn't help but look for threats again. He found none in the giggling girls all dressed in colorful fabrics.

A hand at his back made him jump. Ruhi gasped and Sean turned. And then he gasped.

She was a vision. She didn't wear the traditional white wedding gown. She was an explosion of colors from deep reds to royal blues to lush greens. Her skin was decorated with brown henna in swirling patterns that drew the eye. Sean forgot the danger behind him and focused on the treasure in front of him.

"I'm so sorry," she said. "I snuck up on you again after I said I wouldn't."

He couldn't answer. All he could do was stare.

"Sean? Is everything all right?"

Sean gave himself a shake. "I'm sorry. It's not you, it's me."

Her face fell. Her hand went to her belly, and she began backing away. "Oh, God, no. No, no, no."

"Ruhi? What's wrong? Is it the baby."

"You can't do this to me. It's my wedding day."

"Do what?"

"Break up with me."

"I wouldn't. I'm not."

She paused. Her hand moved from her belly and balled into a fist. "Then what are you on about? Why are you here?"

"I just ... I just got overwhelmed standing out there with all those people."

She stepped back and wrapped her arms around herself. "So you want to call it off?"

Sean held up his hands, moving toward her. "No. I don't want to call it off. I just needed to get away from all of them. I just wish it could be us, just us."

Her face softened, and she dropped her arms from her middle. "I know. I'm sorry." She walked past him, peeking out the door. "But trust me, this is small."

Sean closed the door. He rested his head back

against the frame and allowed himself to gaze down at her. "I just needed a minute alone."

"Were you having flashbacks?"

"Not exactly. My mind starts looking for the danger, and I couldn't stop assessing, even though I know they're all family and friends here to support us."

"So you came and found me?"

He swallowed, but the lump wouldn't move past his throat. So, he came out with it. "You're my safe place. When I came to you for treatment ..." He shrugged. "I just knew I could trust you. Whenever you touched my scar, I didn't jerk away from your touch."

"Unless I sneak up on you." She wiggled her eyebrows.

Sean smiled down at her. He was too tired to try and hide what he was feeling. He knew she saw it when she had a small intake of breath. She lifted her hand slowly and cupped his cheek. He hadn't felt the skin around his wound tug when he smiled. In her hand, he felt no irritation at all.

"I trust you too," she said.

He placed his hand over hers. The connection sent a wave of heat through him, but he felt no danger. Suddenly, he wanted this woman to belong to him. If a piece of paper would do that, then he'd brave the entire crowd in the heat to make it happen.

"Our parents went through a lot of trouble to put this wedding on," he said. "We should honor that."

"True, but we can still do it our way."

"What do you mean?"

Ruhi removed her hand from his face. She laced her fingers with his. "Let's walk each other down the aisle. Together."

CHAPTER TWELVE

Ruhi didn't care about the gasps as she and Sean walked hand and hand down the aisle. There were parts of this ceremony that were traditional and parts that were all Sean and Ruhi. This part, the part where they came into this marriage of their own free will, this was all about them.

Sean's hand engulfed hers, giving her warmth. She squeezed back to show him that she was with him under the gazes of those gathered. She couldn't explain how much it touched her that he'd sought her out during his time of need.

More so it shocked her how hurt she felt when she thought he was breaking up with her. She'd been trying not to get caught up in the preparations of the wedding, but the little girl inside her was bouncing on her toes when she put on her wedding *saree.*

Her breath caught when her mother wrapped her in the fabric. Her hands shook as her sister applied the henna. Her heart raced when she heard Sean's voice at the door.

He'd looked devastatingly handsome from the back as he stood in the entryway. Ruhi hadn't cared about tradition, she wanted to see him. But she'd also wanted him to see her.

She didn't doubt that she'd made the right choice in partner. Sean would be an excellent husband, father, and partner in life.

Already he was discussing things with her. She'd told him some of the details of her five-year plan. Mainly the parts that dealt with the upbringing of the baby. She made no mention of the offer of an exit plan for him at the end of the time period. He'd made no remark about wanting a way out as she told him of her plans.

Instead, he offered her guidance on some of the finer details. He offered input where she was unclear of her direction. He'd stood by her when she put her foot down on somethings their mothers had insisted on in the wedding. He'd also commiserated with her at other points when their mothers asserted their will over their children.

Yes, they were a great team.

And now they were walking down the aisle together to make it official.

It would seem her mother would get another portion of a traditional Indian marriage. Though Ruhi's parents wouldn't be giving her away as they would in the *kanya daan* portion of the ceremony, Sean and Ruhi were performing a version of the *mangal phera* ritual. In that ritual, a couple would join hands and walk circles around a fire. The couple walked hand in hand through their gathered guests toward the sun.

They came to stand before her father who would be officiating the ceremony. Her dad was all smiles as he looked down at his youngest daughter and the man who would promise to take care of her for the rest of their lives.

"Friends, family, canines."

The dogs yipped as her dad announce their breed. The humans chuckled. In the distance, a bird called out a song. It would seem everyone and every beast was excited at the impending union.

"We are gathered here today," her father

continued, "to witness the union of this fine man who will soon be my son in name and deed and my youngest treasure."

Ruhi felt tears sting her eyes as her father gazed down at her with more pride and joy than she'd ever seen. Sean, still holding her hand, gave her fingers a squeeze. Ruhi held onto Sean through much of the ceremony. She found herself unable to meet her father's gaze. Not because she was ashamed at the farce, but because it didn't feel like a farce.

She felt a connection growing to Sean. True, there was no spark of love. But she didn't really miss it.

Finally, she'd found someone who would have her back, someone who would seek her out, someone she could depend on. It was enough. It was more than enough. It was almost, nearly … everything.

"Sean, will you repeat after me?"

Sean turned to Ruhi and repeated the vows her father had written for them. "Ruhi, you are my reason. You are the reason I face the day. You are the reason I brave the night. You are the reason my weaknesses turn to strengths. You are the dream I want to live. I pledge my life to yours, that your dreams become my dreams. No matter where life leads me, I know that your light will always bring me out of the darkness back to you, where I'm meant to be."

Through his hands, Ruhi could feel Sean's pulse racing. Or perhaps it was her own pulse rate. Her father had a gift for vows, but those cut deep, slicing open her heart and pouring out every emotion she ever had. She had to take many deep breaths before she could begin her recitation.

"Sean, I could promise you in sickness and health. I could promise until death do us part. But I won't. You have been sick, and I have brought you back to health. You have seen death and I refused to let you part. For our lives, I will be your healer, I will be your light. Whatever life may bring, I know that I have your loyalty, your protection, your service. And you have mine."

Ruhi watched as her tears were mirrored in Sean's gaze. One escaped and fell down his cheek. She reached up to wipe it away. Her hand stayed, and she cradled the side of his face.

With their written vows to each other complete, they took the *saptapadi*, a vow to support each other in life which required them to take seven steps apart from each other. When they came back together, Sean applied a red powder to the center of Ruhi's forehead and tied a black beaded necklace around her neck. It symbolized that she was now a married woman.

But they weren't done. There was one more tradition that they had to perform. A broom was placed in front of them. This was the African-American tradition of jumping the broom to signify that man and woman were now a union.

Ruhi reached for Sean's hand. They nodded at each other then they jumped over the broom's handle together. On the other side, the two laughed. It was the loudest and most cheerful she'd ever heard Sean.

She liked this side of him. She wanted to see more. And she would in the life that they were about to share.

"You may now kiss your bride," her father said.

There was something weird about having her father tell her to kiss a man. After all the display, and the emotion, and the tears, it was the first time Ruhi had blushed. It was also the one part of the ceremony she hadn't thought to negotiate with her mother.

Ruhi turned to Sean. There was something in his hazel gaze, something bright. Like little tiny sparks.

She stood mesmerized by them as Sean put his hand to her face. Ruhi felt her chin burn where his palm touched. His descent was slow, as though he were allowing her to back out at any moment.

She didn't. She held perfectly still. Those bright tiny lights burned brighter and brighter the closer he came to her. At the last second, Ruhi grew impatient. She closed the distance between them and captured Sean's bottom lip with both of hers.

That's when she knew she was in trouble.

Her heart rate increased. Her stomach did flips. Her palms itched to be filled with more of him.

Sean was soft and firm at the same time. He was sweet and spicy. And he was warm, all warmth. A warmth that infused her body all the way down to her toes.

Five years definitely wouldn't be long enough to get her fill of this comfortable and cozy place. She could stay inside the cradle of his embrace for the rest of her days. And then he broke away.

Sean was close enough that she could lift her head and capture his mouth again. In her heart that was what she wanted to do. But in her head, she knew better.

This was a marriage of practicality, not a love match. Sean was a good guy doing a good thing for her. And he was getting something out of it too.

Now the deed was done. The ink was dry on the marriage certificate. All the rituals had been performed to bond them together for life. There was no backing out now.

CHAPTER THIRTEEN

Sean clenched his hands into fists over and over again. Squeezing hard, he curled his fingers and dug his nails into his palms. He barely registered the pain. There was too much pleasure running through his body. If he didn't get himself under control, he'd surely reach for Ruhi again and repeat that kiss.

It had been chaste by all standards. His fourteen-year-old-self had kissed Cindy Bartlett longer and more firmly than that. He'd perfected the French technique with Lucy Tucker at sixteen, but that too paled in comparison. Just the slightest touch of his lips against Ruhi's, just for a matter of seconds, and he felt the world shift.

With that shift of his inner axis, Sean could take

the brightness of the sun. The clapping of the people gathered, which would have made him wince and retreat into the shadows, didn't bother him so much with Ruhi by his side. He would've never left her side with any potential of danger. But these were all family and friends and they were cheering their union.

Since he couldn't kiss her again, he contented himself with nibbling at his lips, searching out any remaining hint or trace of the momentary sweetness she'd gifted him. He knew that would be the only time they'd kiss. This was to be a marriage of convenience, not one of love. The only passion was on his side.

But it was enough. All he needed was to keep Ruhi by his side where he knew she'd be safe and cared for. Her and her child.

Music began to play and the makeshift dance floor cleared. Ruhi turned to him. Her gaze apologetic for putting him on further display.

Sean didn't care. If it meant holding her in his arms again, he didn't mind at all. He would walk through a minefield just to stand in her shadow.

Sean took Ruhi's hand in his. He gave her a slight tug, and she came to him. She placed her head against his right cheek, over his scar as they began to sway.

Had she done that on purpose? She knew he didn't like it when people stared at his wound. Now they'd be staring at her instead of his scar.

"Thank you," she said, only loud enough for him to hear over the music and the murmur of their guests.

"For what?"

"I don't know if you realize it, but you've just taken on a lot. You see how my mother likes to celebrate. You'll be expected to be at many more of these family celebrations."

"I don't mind," he said. And, truly, he didn't. "I like your parents."

"You've also agreed to become an instant father."

There was that.

Sean had always been good with kids. Until the blast. Now he shied away from them.

But a baby? An infant was innocent. An infant he could help mold and grow.

He would teach this child the right things. Just as his father had taught him. Just as Ruhi's father had taught her. Was that a tickle of hope he felt?

"I won't lie," he said. "I'm nervous about ..."

He looked down at her silk covered belly. His

gaze lifted to meet hers. Ruhi's lips were pursed. Was she holding her breath?

"But we make a great team," he said. "Don't you think?"

Her lips relaxed into a smile. "I do. We do. But you're the one who has to put up with me."

"I like you."

Did he say that too quickly? Was his tone too vehement? Did his hold on her tighten slightly? Had she heard the truth in his statement?

He may have said the word like, but he meant love. Sean loved Ruhi. He had since the first time she'd put her healing hands on his cheek. He knew she didn't feel the same, but she didn't have to.

He would protect her. He would look out for her. He would eliminate any danger before it could get to her. Whether she liked it or not.

"I like you, too," she said.

There was a sparkle in her eyes. It looked to Sean like hope. For the first time in a long time, Sean felt like a hero again. Under her gaze, he was. He would not only slay dragons for this woman, he would not only run into burning buildings for her, he was prepared to change a dirty diaper.

That was true devotion.

"We're gonna be okay, aren't we?" she asked. "This was the best decision for both of us?"

"Yes, I believe that."

"I'm probably going to stink at being a good wife, but I know I'm a good partner."

He didn't believe that. She was good at everything she did because she put her heart into it. But Sean wasn't able to let her know his opinion on that particular topic. They had incoming.

"Uh oh, here comes my dad."

Apparently, the missives were coming from both sides. "And here comes my mom," said Ruhi.

"I'm sorry," they both said in unison.

"I'm cutting in son." Luther Jeffries offered his gnarled, work-worn hand to Sean's new wife. "I want to dance with my beautiful new daughter."

"And I want to dance with my new son," said Mrs. Patel moving into the space Ruhi vacated. "Oh, Luther, the beautiful grandbabies they're going to give us."

"I can't wait to bounce them on my knees."

Both of their parents spoke over Sean and Ruhi. Ruhi's smile wavered. Sean's tightened.

"But we'll have to wait," said Mrs. Patel. "My daughter has a five-year plan, isn't that right, Ruhi?

No babies until you've checked everything off your career list. We'll have to be patient."

Sean watched Ruhi tense in his father's embrace. His father didn't notice. His grin and his pride were so palpable, Sean doubted anything could bring the man down. Sean knew his parents worried about him. They'd been over the moon to learn he was marrying, and marrying Ruhi to boot. They'd met and liked his nurse last year.

"You dance beautifully, Mrs. Patel," said Sean, twirling the older woman in his arms. His father could be distracted. But he doubted the psychologist's wife would turn so easily. And so he turned her away from her daughter.

"Oh, my dear, you must call me Mommy. All my children do."

"Yes, ma'am—Mommy."

"I want you to know I truly don't think my daughter could've done better than you. My husband has a lot of respect for you, as do all the men here. I know you're a man of faith, though a private one. Still, I wish you would join us at church. Let people see how beautiful your spirit is, both inside and out."

"Thank you, Mrs. -Mommy. I promise I'm going to make your daughter very happy."

"The secret to a good marriage is honesty. You be honest with each other and you'll last a lifetime."

"Yes, ma'am." Sean twirled the woman again as he answered.

Mrs. Patel frowned as she came out of the turn. Oh, no. Did she suspect something? Did she know they were already enmeshed in a lie? "Yes, what ...?"

Oh. "Yes, Mommy."

CHAPTER FOURTEEN

The party lasted into the night. Between the gospel and soul music from Sean's side of the family, to the Bollywood tunes from her side of the aisle, the partying, the praising, and the dancing, it didn't look like it was going to stop until dawn. But Ruhi was exhausted before midnight.

Before she knew it, Sean's hand was at her low back, and he was steering her away from the festivities. He said their good nights as they went. All Ruhi had to do was lean into his shoulder, which she did.

She was his wife, after all. This was definitely a perk. She didn't have to stand on her own, she would be expected to lean on him a bit, if she were tired. And she was tired.

Between the ceremony, the cake, the curried chicken, the fried chicken, the barbecue chicken, and rice and potato salad, she was ready to be rolled down the lane. And there was still the fact of the growing being inside her who zapped her energy every other second.

Luckily, zapping energy was all the baby was doing. Ruhi had been able to eat and keep the food down. But having to constantly tell small lies and stick to a story made her mentally exhausted. Everyone wanted to know the story of how she and Sean fell in love.

They'd concocted a simple enough story that stuck as closely to the truth as possible. After her last break up, Sean was there to pick up the pieces. They realized they had feelings for each other that had been growing over the year they'd known each other. They knew that it was right, so they decided not to wait.

Each person they told the story to bought it hook, line, and sinker. Though the soldiers assumed the speedy marriage was due to the zoning issue. Her side of the family didn't have any issues with quick marriages. Ruhi and Sean had thought his parents would need more convincing, but they had met Ruhi before and were thrilled at the union.

Telling the story wasn't a real hardship. What truly bothered Ruhi was having to fib about was her love for Sean. She liked Sean, more and more each day. But love?

She wanted to tell everyone that that emotion wasn't in the cards for her. Michael had been right. She'd never felt that spark for him. She'd never felt it for anyone. Now she had to pretend it was there with Sean.

Sean deserved a spark. He deserved a romance. He deserved a girl who would look at him with stars in her eyes. He'd never get that with Ruhi.

An even worse thought entered her mind. What if he sparked with someone one day during their marriage? What if it was Ruhi who stood in the way.

But she was too tired to think of that. Sean's hand at the small of her back was far too comforting. All she wanted to do was stay in the crook of his arm and rest. Before she knew it, they were back at his place.

Sean unlocked the door to his cabin. She'd been inside briefly today, but only long enough to drop off her necessities. The rest of her things were still back in her apartment. This house was still foreign to her.

She'd visited Dylan's cabin to have dinner with him and Maggie shortly after their wedding. She'd visited Fran and Eva's home when Rosalee had come down with a bad cold. She'd had no reason to be in the other guy's homes. Sean, Reed, and Xavier each had lived alone in their two-bedroom bunkhouses. Now one of those bunkhouses was her home.

"I set up an office in the breakfast nook for you," he said turning on a light.

In the small space, the illumination showed a small desk with a computer and a filing cabinet where a breakfast nook must've once been. It was cozy and quaint and so thoughtful.

"Sean ... thank you."

"There are only two bedrooms, but I figure that's fine for now and the baby's first year. We can decide if we want to add on to this house or build something new in the future."

The future. When she was a mother. All of her plans were out of whack. She still had more revisions to make with her five-year plan. She'd have to consult Sean in those plans. But she definitely wasn't doing it tonight. She just wanted to rest.

"You're tired," said Sean. He steered her down the hall. "It's been a long day. We can talk about this at another time when you're thinking clearly. We'll do what you think is best."

"Me?"

"Of course. I know we agreed to be equal partners, but this affects you most. You take the lead. I'm behind whatever you want to do."

His hand was still at the small of her back. It was the only thing holding her up. Standing in front of his spare bedroom door, Ruhi turned and wrapped Sean up in her arms. Slowly, tentatively, his arms came around her.

Belatedly, Ruhi wondered if she'd overstepped her bounds? Was she being too affectionate with him? Too familiar?

"And there's something else," he said as his cheek rested on the top of her head. "I think the balance of duties will be skewed for a bit with you being pregnant twenty-four-seven for the next year. So, I'm taking on a majority of the household chores. I insist."

Ruhi didn't know what to say. Sean was practically the man of her dreams, offering her everything she ever thought she wanted in a relationship. Except they weren't in a relationship.

"Thank you," she said into his chest. She was tempted to fall asleep with her cheek resting against the cushion of his right pec. "I couldn't do any of this without you."

"I told you, I wouldn't have come through this past year without you. I'm in your debt."

He pulled away from her then. She wanted to whimper in protest as his warmth fell away from her. The moment his hand left her back, Ruhi felt weak. But she didn't dare show it.

With just these few gestures Sean proved to be the best boyfriend she'd ever had. And once again, he was not her boyfriend. But he was something better.

He was her partner.

She just wished it was acceptable for him to lie down next to her with his hand supporting her lower back until she fell asleep. But that wasn't part of the deal. So Ruhi closed the door to the spare bedroom behind her and found herself as she always was; alone and on her own.

CHAPTER FIFTEEN

"Sean, you don't have to do this."

Sean gazed down at his new wife. Her lips were pursed to one side of her mouth. It was her thinking face. He'd found the facial gesture endearing when she'd first started treating him. He'd soon learned it was the expression she made when she was unsure of something and would have to go and consult a chart or a medical text.

"This is now part of my responsibility," he said.

Ruhi pulled her car into the doctor's office and put the car in park. Sean had loved the surprised look on her face when he'd opened up the driver's side door for her and then hopped into the passenger seat. He knew Ruhi liked her independence, and Sean had no need to take any of it away from her.

He didn't think letting a woman into the driver's seat, or a man cooking for a woman, or either of them picking up a dustpan made him any less of a man. Real men did what needed to be done. His father had taught him that.

And his mother's bark was not worse than her bite. His mother's bite stung. Though Sean had only felt her bite a few times in his life, because he rarely misbehaved.

He liked strong women. They were overflowing in his immediate as well as his extended family. He'd also been surrounded by that particular breed of women while in the service. The only people threatened by strong women were weak people. Weak men and weak women.

Sean didn't doubt his strength. He and Ruhi had spent the weekend in relative quiet. The guys had moved her items from the apartment to the ranch. She'd unpacked while Sean helped. He enjoyed putting up her things in their shared space.

No one commented on the fact that they had separate rooms. Though Sean was certain when their parents came to visit they would have questions. But that would hold for some time.

Though he'd had no problem with Ruhi driving, he did hop out of the car to hand her out of the driver's side. He was an evolved man, but he was also a gentleman.

"I just don't want you to feel obligated to do this stuff," she said.

"If I had to go to the doctor's outside of the ranch, would you come with me?"

"That's different. I'm your nurse."

"I'm your husband."

That remark made her hold her tongue. He hadn't said that out loud. This was the first time, and he liked the sound of it.

Sean placed his hand at the small of Ruhi's back, preparing to guide her across the street. He looked left and right for any signs of danger as he waited for her next protest. There were no cars coming in either direction. There also was no argument coming from her lips.

Instead, she leaned into him and allowed him to guide her into the building. As much as he liked this strong woman beside him who could stand on her own, he loved it when she took solace in his embrace. He chalked up her lack of fight to the pregnancy. He'd be certain to take advantage for the next eight months.

Sean kept his arm around her as they waited in the waiting room. He joined her in the exam room, turning his back as she undressed to step into a hospital gown. The doctor joined them shortly after.

Sean had been surprised to find that the OB/GYN Ruhi had chosen was a man. He would've been certain that a modern woman such as herself would want another strong female delivering her firstborn. Ruhi had shrugged and said she wasn't a sexist.

It was her first visit with the OB/GYN, so the doctor didn't know any of their particulars and that included their relationship.

"We're recently married," Ruhi said. "Just this weekend."

"By my calculations, you're six weeks pregnant," said the doctor. His gaze went from Ruhi to Sean.

"That's about right," said Sean. He watched the doctor's shoulders relax. Sean wondered how many times that math had broken couples up?

"Would you like to hear the baby's heartbeat?" asked the doctor.

Ruhi hesitated. She looked to Sean. Sean took her hand in his. He lifted his brow. The decision was hers. Ruhi turned to the doctor and nodded.

The doctor lifted the hospital gown to reveal

Ruhi's belly. Sean felt he should avert his gaze. But he was her husband, and for all intents and purposes, the one who put the baby in there. So, he looked.

There was a translucent splat of jelly on her flat belly. Then the doctor pulled out what looked like a back massager. He put the bulbous head on her belly and began moving it around. Both Ruhi's and the doctor's gazes turned to a black and white monitor. Sean didn't look away from his wife's belly. Not until he heard it.

The sound pounded into his ears like a soldier's march. It crackled like the interference in a two-way headset. He expected the screams of trapped civilians to come next, followed by the pants of desperation of those he could not save trying to snatch his attention away.

Sean felt his palms go sweaty. His jaw clenched tighter and tighter as the PTSD began to tug at him. Instead of the panic that would set his trigger finger itchy, something tugged at his hand.

"Sean?" Ruhi's fingers curled into his palm, grounding him back into reality. "Do you hear it?"

Slowly the pounding softened. The crackling dissipated. The pulsing vibrations evened out until they became a single note. A delicate beating.

This was not the sound of death. It was the sound of life. A new life that was growing.

It was so small. So precious. So delicate.

For the first time in a long time, Sean wanted to run toward the pounding. He wanted to protect it, to hold it to him, to save it.

This heartbeat, this life, was the work of another man. But Sean was stepping up to the plate. He would help this child grow. He would help mold it. He would be its hero.

CHAPTER SIXTEEN

The missed period, the morning sickness, the positive pregnancy test, all those hadn't truly made Ruhi know she was pregnant. Hearing her baby's heartbeat made it all real. That tiny little sound is what let her know that she was a mom.

She wasn't going to be a mom. It had already happened. There was a living, breathing, beating life inside her. It was growing fast and it was depending on her.

The realization clicked the second she heard her child's heartbeat. The second she saw the monitor come to life with the evidence deep in her womb. And when it did, all her carefully thought out plans went out the window.

This was a lifetime job. In one year, she'd be holding a baby in her arms. In five years, she'd be doing the same. Any job, any mission, any adventure would have to involve and revolve around her child.

And Sean.

Ruhi had fought so hard to prove she was independent her whole life. But in an instant, she couldn't imagine the rest of her life without these two beings. One she hadn't met yet. One she'd known for a short while who'd become integral to her wellbeing.

She handed Sean her car keys as they exited the doctor's office. He walked around and opened the passenger side door. She'd never liked that gesture, a man opening doors for a woman as though he was the key to her passage through. When Sean held the door open for her, or pulled out her seat for her, or held out his hand to her, it made her feel that he was making way for her to experience something she'd never known before. And best of all, she knew she wouldn't do it alone.

Ruhi stepped into the passenger side of her car. She settled into the seat. She strapped in as her partner in life took the wheel.

"Are you hungry? Tired?" Sean asked.

Ruhi shrugged. She was content to let him figure

out the agenda for the rest of the day. She didn't doubt he'd get her exactly what she needed. And so she closed her eyes. When she opened them, they were back at the ranch. She smelled spicy foods, but she was still inside the car. A bag of take-out sat in the back seat.

Ruhi smiled. It was exactly what she needed. Rest and food.

She waited for Sean to come around to the passenger side and hand her out. With the food in one hand, she took his other hand. Once she was out of the car, he rested his free hand on the small of her back. Inside their home, Sean settled her on the couch with a TV dinner tray. He pulled the food out and placed the cartons before her.

"You're spoiling me," she said.

He only smiled. "You've taken care of me so long, it's time someone took care of you. Just for the day. You can boss me around tomorrow."

"Am I bossy?"

Sean paused, looking down at her. "You're assertive. You know what you want. And you're smart. Most of the time I assume you've thought things through so I'm happy to follow along. That's important to a soldier. You want to trust the person in your squad. You're in my squad now."

"I trust you, too."

His lips parted, but he said nothing. Ruhi's heart beat in her ear. Her cheeks flooded with warmth. The moment was so ripe for a kiss.

If they had that kind of relationship. Which they didn't have. Which they couldn't have.

The last thing Ruhi wanted was another man telling her he felt no spark for her. Sean wasn't in love with her. They'd known each other for a year. If love was going to show up between them, it would've done it months ago.

What was between them was a warm and cozy friendship. She could lean on him. Better yet, he had proven he wouldn't buckle under the weight or turn from her if the load got too heavy.

She'd kissed men that she hadn't felt a spark with, hoping something would kindle and grow. When she'd kissed Sean there had been no spark. Only a sense of rightness. He was the right man for her.

Maybe kissing didn't have to stay off the table in this relationship? Maybe they could enjoy each other physically someday. She certainly enjoyed his embraces. Just the simple nearness of him.

He was young and virile. Surely he couldn't go without the comfort of a woman for the rest of his life. They had time. She would broach this subject in the future. Maybe after the baby was born.

"I know you have the rest of the day off," he said. "But I'm going to go check on a few things around the ranch. I won't be long."

"Okay."

He leaned down toward her. Ruhi held her breath. Her mouth watered as he came nearer. Maybe the physical things could start between them sooner?

Ruhi tilted up her head. Sean's lips didn't make it past her forehead. Warmth spread through her as he planted a light kiss between her brow. Not an explosion. Just a pleasant hum of heat.

"Call me if you need anything," he said when he pulled away.

"I'll be fine," she smiled.

He rose and headed out the door. Ruhi watched after him. Her mouth watered even more as she watched the backside of him go out the door. She still felt that burning hunger when the door clicked shut. Finally, she registered the buffet before she attacked the food.

She was partway through her second carton of takeout when her phone rang. When she looked at the caller ID she dropped her fork.

It was Michael.

What did he want? It didn't matter. She didn't want to deal with him now.

But she should answer. She should tell him about the baby. He had a right to know. Even though she was certain he'd shuck his responsibilities.

By the time she reached for the phone, it had stopped ringing. Maybe he'd call back. If he did, she'd tell him. If not, she'd call him later.

By the time she'd cleaned the takeout boxes, Michael hadn't called back. Sean hadn't returned either. Ruhi didn't feel like waiting for either of them and so she took a nap instead.

CHAPTER SEVENTEEN

Sean aimed to rush through his chores and get back to his wife. His last sight of Ruhi tucked in on the couch gazing up at him was all he could think of. He was having a hard time convincing himself that there was nothing between them with the way she'd looked up at him. Perhaps, the more time they spent together, the more this could become something that resembled a real marriage.

With Scar at his heels and Ruhi on his mind, Sean grabbed the liquid fertilizer instead of the weed killer to tame the wayward grass in an overgrown patch of field and didn't realize his mistake until Scar ran away whining. That's when Sean looked down to see that half of the patch was covered with the growth treatment. He caught himself as he grabbed the chicken feed just as he entered the horse stalls. Finally, he decided it was best if he stayed away from the animals and headed to work with the inanimate objects on the ranch.

Luckily, the addition of the youth program had lessened the amount of work he had to do. But with Dylan and Fran focused on the boys in the program, that did leave Sean on his own to handle some of the duties that would be faster if he had another adult at hand.

Xavier and Reed were off in the city picking up supplies. The three women who lived on the ranch each had taken on their own duties. Maggie worked alongside the trainers to take care of the animals. Eva, who was excellent with numbers, took over the books. And Sarai was hard at work on the ranch's website.

Sean grabbed a hammer and some nails. There was always a fence that needed mending on a ranch. It was tougher to do the work on his own, but at least he wouldn't accidentally hammer another person's thumb to a piece of wood in his distracted state. With the pesticides back on the shelf, Scar returned to join him.

The sun was behind the clouds and stayed off his

back as Sean worked. Scar quickly fell asleep on a patch of grass. In the shade, Sean was able to hide from any memories of the explosion. So, when he heard footsteps approaching he wasn't caught off guard. He assumed it was one of his brothers coming to give him a hand. The coughing fit that accompanied the footfalls told Sean he was wrong.

"Aren't you supposed to be with your group?" Sean asked the kid.

James bent down to scratch Scar behind her ears. "I just slow them down. I don't understand why we have to be a unit anyway. I just want to work with the animals."

Sean stood and the kid kicked at a stone with his worn shoes. He shoved his hands into pockets which rode the hem of his jeans up enough to show his socks above his ankles. His shirt had one too many stains that looked like they were older than the kid. Was there no one taking care of this kid?

"Come give me a hand," said Sean. "You take one end of the rail, and I'll take the other."

Sean still wound up taking most of the weight, but it was less wieldy than when he was holding the wood by himself. He quickly nailed in one side and joined the kid on the other.

"I could do that on my own," he said. "But with

two people it moves easier and faster."

"Yeah," said the kid. "But you can ride a horse by yourself."

"When we take you out to herd the cattle, you can't do that by yourself."

"Can't you use a dog?"

"You would have to train the dog. Then you and the dog would be a unit."

James pursed his lips at that. He shoved his hands back into his pockets. Sean clearly saw the outline of each of his fingers in the threadbare fabric.

He made a mental note to ask Sarai to look into getting some clothes for kids. He knew the former model still had some contacts in the fashion world. After the kids' hesitancy to take charity money for the prescription, Sean assumed that James wouldn't take the hand out of clothing. Sean had managed to sneak some cash into the kid's backpack the last time they were on the ranch. It was enough to pay for the prescription. Sean hoped the kid had used it for that.

"You need someone to watch your back," Sean said. "The friends you make will watch your back. But you need to watch theirs too."

Speak of the little devil, Maurice made his way

through the fields towards them. He didn't look pleased as he came up to James. "Hey, you just left me back there."

"Sorry," said James. He kicked at a pebble on the ground and shoved his hands deeper in his pockets. "I was just giving Specialist Jeffries a hand."

"We're supposed to be stacking the hay bales together. I turned around, and you were gone."

"The hay was making me sneeze and ..." James opened his mouth and let out a string of wheezing coughs. He wheezed so hard he was sucking down air in strained gasps.

Sean wasn't sure if he should go to the kid? Were there rules about touching the kids, even if only to pat them on the back? What if he had to give the kid CPR?

As Sean hesitated, Maurice stepped up and rubbed his hand on James's back. "I thought you went to the doctors."

"I did."

"Did your dad get you the medicine?"

"Yeah, I just forgot to take it." James kicked at another pebble. "I will when I go home."

He shoved his hands in his pockets and kept his head down as he turned to go. Scar trailed after her new ear-scratching friend. Maurice looked to Sean and shrugged before turning to follow James. Sean knew bronchitis could last weeks, months even. But with medication, it should be getting better and not worse.

Clearly, the kid didn't have the medication. If it had been in his system for a couple of days now, he'd be improving. How could this father not do what was necessary to take care of his kid? If Sean had heard that cough come from his kid, he'd move heaven and earth to make it stop.

The reason these kids were all here was because their parents neglected them on some level. Why else would they be acting up or getting bad grades or falling ill? It was criminal to treat a child with so much neglect, nearly as bad as indoctrinating them to harm others.

"For a newlywed, you don't look too happy."

Sean turned to see Fran walk up.

"It's a crime how some of these parents are treating their kids," said Sean, motioning to the kids still walking in the distance. "When our child gets here, I'll move heaven and earth to make sure they have everything they need."

"Your child? Wait. Is Ruhi pregnant?"

Sean froze. His tongue had loosened in his anger. There was no way he could take that outburst back, or distract Fran with something else. But that wasn't even the worst to come.

"But you two only just … Oh."

Fran had obviously done the math in his head and came to the baby daddy conclusion without Maury Povich's blood test results.

Fran whistled, tilting his head back to the sky. Then he dropped his gaze to Sean's, a serious look on his face. "I know how you feel about her. But another man's child?"

"He left her," said Sean. "What kind of man does that when a woman is carrying his child? I'll be here for them both. I'll be the best husband and father."

The title role of Best Father he wasn't worried about. He'd had great examples of that in his life. The title role of Best Husband? There he worried. He was married to the woman he was in love with, but he had to hide the depth of his feelings on a daily basis. Well, at least the pregnancy was one less thing he had to hide.

"Look, Fran, we're keeping it quiet."

"Of course." Fran nodded.

But Sean knew that by the time he got home it would be all over the ranch. Including to the medical offices where Ruhi's dad would be tomorrow. And then they'd all start doing the math.

CHAPTER EIGHTEEN

Ruhi felt exhausted in her dream. She knew that morning had turned to afternoon because she could feel the sun on her cheek. But she was cold. Why was it so cold?

Her eyes refused to open. Until a trail of heat touched her brow. Her awareness tracked that heat. Across her forehead, down her jaw, back behind her ear. Then it was gone.

Ruhi blinked her eyes open in search of the heat and found Sean. His brown skin positively glowed in the afternoon sunlight. His hazel eyes were like stars shining solely for her. She wanted to curl up and burrow deep in his feather-light embrace. But he jerked his hand away from her face, and he looked down, shutting off her view of the twin stars.

She blinked a few more times. Light was all around him, strands of sunlight coming through the window, like sparks. It had been Sean. He'd warmed her through with the slightest touch.

"I'm sorry to wake you," he said. "You looked so peaceful."

"It was. I am."

He lifted his lashes to look at her. And there it was again, that light in his eyes. Fireworks bubbled in her belly. But she didn't feel sick.

Lightheaded, yes.

Dizzy, a bit.

Breathless, definitely.

These weren't pregnancy symptoms. These were the things people said about falling in love at first sight. But that wasn't happening. Not between her and Sean.

She'd known Sean for a year. If anything were to spark between them, it would've happened by now. So, this couldn't be love.

Could it?

It was the first time she'd seen him in this light. Before it had always been under the harsh glare of fluorescent light in the clinic. He'd never been looking down at her. She'd always been looking up at him or eye to eye as she examined him. But her heart was doing funny, fluttery things under his gaze.

Ruhi knew love happened immediately as well as over time. It had just never happened like that to anyone she knew, certainly not anyone in her family. Everyone talked about it being in an instant, or shortly after the first meeting.

She' been in too many relationships where she stuck around to wait and see if something would catch. It never did. Hadn't she given up on that?

She had. But something was happening inside her. Something itched. Something burned. One moment it wasn't there. And the next it was.

"Ruhi, we have to talk."

In another instant, she felt sick. The lightheadedness, the dizziness, the breathlessness swung across a spectrum that pointed to nausea.

"The cat's out of the bag," he said. "Or rather, the bun is out of the oven."

"What?"

Ruhi sat up. The change in altitude sent her head reeling. She reached out for something to hold onto, and Sean was there.

He wrapped his hand around hers, and she felt grounded, but not secure. Sean slid onto the couch beside her, and like a magnet, her body snapped into place inside his embrace. If he was breaking up with her, he'd have to figure out how to pry her out of this spot because she just didn't have the energy or the inclination to move.

Instead of pushing her away, his arms wrapped around her. One came to rest at her low back. The other cradled her head.

"How are you feeling?" he asked.

"Warm," Ruhi said into his chest. "I was so cold. And now I'm warm."

"I'm so sorry about that. I keep the thermostat low in here. I thought the blanket would be enough to keep you warm."

"It was. But this is better." Since he wasn't pushing her away, she decided to snuggle deeper into his chest.

They sat quietly for a long moment. Sean stroked his hand in circles on her low back. Ruhi took slow breaths that filled her with his scent. If this was how he broke bad news, she was willing to get used to it. But the moment he started talking her stomach tied in knots again.

"I have bad news," he began.

Ruhi took a deep breath. Slowly she lifted her head to look her fake husband in the eye. But she did not leave his embrace. He owed her some comfort if he was about to pull the rug out from under her.

"Fran guessed that you're pregnant, and he figured it wasn't mine. I'm sure everyone knows by now, and your father will likely find out tomorrow when he's here."

It took Ruhi a moment to comprehend what he was saying. She was so focused on listening for the familiar breakup phrases. Her mind went over Sean's words again and again. When she couldn't pick out a single break up cliché, her heart settled. Her breathing evened. Her head cleared.

"You're not breaking up with me?" she clarified.

Sean blinked. The light in his eyes dimmed and then burned brighter. "Breaking up with you?"

He had to force the words out. They sounded so foreign on his tongue. Ruhi could see him turning his words over and over in his mind just as she'd turned over what he'd said to her.

"Never," he concluded.

"Never?" she asked.

He unwrapped himself from her and slid from the couch. Before she knew what was happening, Sean was down on his knees. He reached for her hands. Ruhi was so stunned at the turn of events that she gave them both over.

"There's something you need to know," he said. "Something I should've told you before we got married. I'm ... I'm in love ..."

"You're in love with someone else?" She finished the sentence for him. She forced the words out with a choke. She knew it.

"Ruhi. I'm in love with you. I have been since my first appointment with you."

"With me?"

Sean nodded, his gaze open and vulnerable. As those flecks twinkled at her, she saw it. He'd looked at her like that countless times. How had she not seen it?

"I didn't want to make you uncomfortable, but you should know it if we're going to be together. There should be no secrets. I was in a dark place when I came to you. I felt my heart come back to life when you lifted my chin to heal my wound."

"I was so focused on healing you, I didn't look at you. I didn't realize it was even there."

"And now?"

"Now ..." She lifted her hand to his cheek. "Now, I see it. Now, I feel it."

She cupped his face with both her hands, running her thumbs over his cheeks. She was close enough to taste the warm spice of his breath.

"A spark."

Ruhi leaned down as Sean pulled her to him. Their lips touched softly, but it was an explosion of sensation. The impact of his bottom lip against her top stole her breath. When he tilted her head to gain more access, Ruhi's entire world went off its axis. She felt her world shatter as Sean's lips claimed her own. She felt put back together as he held her firmly inside his arms.

It was a new state of being. She no longer felt that she was an independent woman. She'd become more. She'd grown and was now a rock solid unit.

CHAPTER NINETEEN

Warmth surrounded him. He felt the heat radiating from his chest. There was lightness in his limbs and a tingling in his hands. Absent was the cold, steel hardness of a weapon.

Sean waited for the panic to settle in. He was defenseless in a dark, hot place. But his heart was calm.

The warmth moved up to his face. He felt it creep and crawl through the grooves of his cheek where the wound lay. In the nightmares, he never had the scar. Not until he woke up and ran his hand over his face. That was the way he knew he was out of the dream world and back to the harsh reality.

The heat left his face and quickly migrated to his

back. This was more like the regular nightmares, the ones that mirrored the horror of what he'd faced back in a combat zone. The pounding in his ears started next.

Only, there wasn't just a deep, hollowness with the drumming sound. It went from a single heartbeat to multiple and back again. From out of the darkness, the sound of cries rose. The high-pitched wail of an infant's cry quickly drowned out all the other voices.

Sean inhaled to calm his heart's beating, trying to gain control of himself. This was a dream, a nightmare. He just had to wake up, to open his eyes.

But the bodies fell around him. The child's cry rang louder in his ears. The trilling wail of distress threatened to break his entire being in two.

He managed to open his eyes, but he was still in the dream. Shards of light broke through. It was the light of the flame. Red, hot, angry sparks leaped out at him. They lashed at his skin, licked up his spine, smacked him in the face.

But he didn't fall. He couldn't. He knew the only way out of the dream was to find Xavier. But the man's prone body was nowhere to be found. Then he saw it.

At the end of the tunnel, he saw Ruhi, a child in her arms. Her child. Their child. His child.

The child screamed in distress. Ruhi called out in fear. She was calling his name.

Desperation tore through Sean like a missive finding its target. Sean pumped his legs. But the faster he moved, the farther away they appeared to get. And still, Ruhi called out his name.

He was close. He was so close. A dark figure moved into view behind Ruhi and the baby.

The figure was small, half Ruhi's size. It was a young boy. The boy wore what Sean knew to be a suicide vest. Tears streamed down the kid's face.

"Sean?"

Sean had to act. The boy's life or his family's lives He'd never wanted to make this decision again. But here it was, and he was hesitating again.

"Sean?"

He felt the cold, hard steel of a gun in his hands. He lifted the weapon. He cocked the gun. He aimed and—

"Sean, it's a dream. Wake up."

His eyes tore open. His hands reached out, searching for his weapon. Instead of steel, he found flesh.

Ruhi's eyes were wide. Her breaths came in

anxious pants. Her face ashen in the dim moonlight. Her palms faced him, fingers straining upward in a stop motion. Sean saw his own fingers wrapped around her wrists.

She was frightened. She was afraid. Of him. The nightmare was nothing to this reality. This was hell.

"Oh, God. Did I hurt you?"

Sean released her hands and scooted away from her. They were still on the couch in the living room. He remembered that after their shared kiss, they relaxed back on the couch, content to stay in each other's arms. They both must've fallen asleep.

"No," she said. "You didn't hurt me. Are you okay?"

He didn't take her word for it. He reached over and turned on a table lamp. Under the fluorescent light, he did a visual scan of her body, searching for any wounds he may have inflicted on her while the nightmare had him.

He found none. This time. "I could've hurt you."

"You never would." Ruhi lifted her hand to his face.

"On purpose—never. By accident, that's very possible."

"I know about the nightmares, Sean. But just now, you were reaching for me, and I'm right here."

Sean looked down at his hands. "I grabbed your wrists."

She shook her head. "When you woke up. But before that, you were pulling me toward you. Holding me tight. I think you were protecting me."

Ruhi brushed her thumb over his cheek. Then her index finger lifted his chin so that he met her stare. There was no fear in her gaze.

There was warmth in her brown eyes. Compassion laced her heavy lashes. There was also a spark of something else at the corner of her eyelids. For the first time in a long time, Sean wished he had a match to fuel that flicker into a flame.

When he'd confessed his feelings to her, she hadn't said she loved him back. And that was fine. A spark was fine. Though he'd kept himself in the dark cold for so long, he did know how to feed a fire. He was happy to spend the rest of his life adding kindling to Ruhi's heart in hopes to make love grow.

"I know better than to startle you," she said. "But I needed you to know that I was safe. That I was with you."

Sean's chin fell to his chest. Not out of shame. Out of exhaustion. He'd been holding himself so tightly together. But she'd unraveled him in just a second.

"I know your PTSD is real and has real consequences. But we'll face them together."

"Heat's a trigger," said Sean.

"Oh, that's why it's so cold in here all the time." She shrugged. "I'll wear thermal underwear."

Thinking about Ruhi's underwear only made him get hot under the collar. "We're not sleeping together. Not until I get a handle on these nightmares."

"Oh." Her shoulders sank, and she let out a weary sigh. "Great."

She was disappointed. That was a great sign. "I want to," Sean insisted.

"Me too."

She was kneeling on the couch facing him. Both of her knees brushed up against his thighs. It would be so easy to pull her onto his lap. But not yet.

"I just need to be sure," he said. "I need to trust myself with you."

"So you're asking me to wait a while?"

"I promise to be worth the wait."

He did pull her close then. Not onto his lap. He pulled her chest against his heart.

This time, Sean took Ruhi's face in his hands. He cupped her chin, rubbing his thumb over the bottom lip he planned to capture again and again between his own lips.

Ruhi's breath was warm against his palm. Her heat and her nearness were having a triggering effect on him. Only he was far from hell. This was heaven.

Sean tilted Ruhi's face. He locked in on his target. His aim was true as he closed in on his quarry.

The chime of a cell phone broke them apart. Sean glanced down at Ruhi's phone on the coffee table and froze. He saw her ex-boyfriend's face. Followed by a text that read. "Got your message. You up?"

"Why is your ex sending you a booty call text message at one in the morning?"

Ruhi shut her eyes to try to regain balance. She was caught between a haze of want and a fog of annoyance. What she wanted was for Sean to finish what he'd started and kiss her senseless as he'd done before she'd fallen asleep safe in his arms. She wanted to test the bounds of his resolve to keep her at arm's distance while they sorted these nightmares. Ruhi had every plan to conduct those tests while inside his embrace.

When he'd been caught in the snare of his dark dreams, her first and only instinct was to let him know that she was there for him. The way he'd been there for her this whole time. Sean had never once wavered since he'd come to her aid. He'd never stepped back as she increasingly came to lean on him.

Ruhi was determined to do the same for him. Whatever he needed to manage his PTSD, she would do. As long as it didn't include leaving the comfort of his arms, or giving up his heart-melting kisses. Those were all non-negotiable.

Unfortunately, Michael had impeccable timing. She'd called him earlier in the day before Sean had come home. It had taken him all day to respond.

Come to think of it, he never got back to her immediately during their relationship. She'd always felt like an afterthought when it came to his daily agenda. She'd often been pushed aside when a new opportunity presented itself.

Still, Michael was now and would forever be the father of her child. She had to set the record straight with him. But first, she had to tell her husband the full truth.

"Sean, there's something Michael and I need to talk about. Something you and I have to talk about first."

"About the baby?"

Ruhi nodded.

Sean released her face, but he didn't move away from her. He rested his hand on the back of the couch. With his free hand, he took Ruhi's hand in his. "Do you think he's changed his mind? Do you think he wants to be a part of our child's life now?"

Our child. How had she not seen the amazingness of this man for an entire year? He'd come to her every week for a year.

She'd stared directly at his face, straight into his eyes. She'd seen his strength; she'd seen his resilience. She knew he was trustworthy and honest. But that mutual respect that shone through as he regarded her, that immediate acceptance without judgment, those qualities finally pierced through her prescriptive mind and lodged inside her heart.

Ruhi wished she'd opened her eyes to him last year. She wished she'd allowed him into her heart sooner. Then this would be their child in spirit as well as in blood.

But she couldn't hide the facts. By now everyone on the ranch would know. They'd know she was pregnant, and Sean wasn't the father.

Her parents would know by morning, and would likely be crushed that they weren't the first to know. She'd screwed it all up. Even worse, Michael, the child's father, would be the very last to know.

"Michael can't change his mind until he has all the information," she said.

Sean's brows drew in confusion. But his gaze remained patient. The small smile on his lips still spoke of trust.

"I never told him I was pregnant."

Now he pulled away from her. His fingers released hers. His arm that had lain on the back of the couch pulled out of the half embrace. "You never told him about the baby?"

"I found out I was pregnant after we broke up and he was preparing to leave the country. He was already sleeping with someone else when I tried to tell him."

"Ruhi..." He didn't look at her. He looked down at his hands. The hands that had been holding her a moment ago, bringing her into his embrace, into his protection, into his heart.

"I know, I know. I was just so humiliated. But I called him again this morning. He's just now getting back to me."

Sean lifted his gaze. His hazel eyes dark, his jaw tight. "And if he wants to get back with you?"

"Trust me, he doesn't."

"Do you want him to want you?" Sean wrung his

hands together, clenching and unclenching his fingers into fists.

"No." Ruhi laughed at that. "Not at all."

She had wanted Michael to want her. But being wanted by Sean was far better. So why was Sean getting up from the couch?

"Sean?" Ruhi rose to join him.

"A child needs both their parents."

"This child will have a mother and a father regardless of what Michael decides."

"I thought I was stepping into a vacant spot."

"You did," she insisted. "You stepped into my heart."

Sean's gaze raked over her. Ruhi felt exposed under the heat of his perusal. She felt her soul was laid bare as her husband judged her past decisions and present actions.

Sean didn't have a wide range of facial expressions, but Ruhi knew his face so well. He was hurt. He was confused. He was disappointed.

"Sean?"

"It's late. You should get your rest."

He held his hand out to her. But when Ruhi reached her fingers to his, he ducked his hand around her back. All week long when he'd rested his hand at the small of her back, she'd felt anchored, grounded. Now she only felt the weight of the world pulling her down.

Sean walked her to her bedroom door. He turned the knob and handed her inside. "Good night, Ruhi."

"Sean?"

"Let's talk in the morning."

And with that, he shut the door with a quiet snick. A moment later she heard the same small snick of his door shutting her out. He hadn't said the words, but Ruhi felt that somehow they'd just broken up.

CHAPTER TWENTY-ONE

The sound of his name on her lips reverberated in his ears again and again. It muted the sounds of screams and cries of his nightmare. It left him feeling cold. He couldn't close his eyes in bed. But keeping them open he could only stare at the shut door.

He'd had her in his arms. He'd tasted her lips. He'd admitted to his feelings and she'd reciprocated. It had been everything he'd ever wanted. And it was all based on a lie.

Not the lie they told together. That lie was different. It had been for the greater good. They'd done it to protect the child. Only now it might have been for nothing.

What if Michael wanted to be a part of the baby's life?

Ruhi had said she didn't want her ex back. But if he wanted to be a part of the baby's life, she couldn't exclude him. So where did that leave Sean?

Whether he'd known about the baby or not, Michael had tossed Ruhi aside when he'd dumped her. Sean knew the breakup hadn't been consensual. Most weren't. She clearly hadn't expected it, hadn't wanted it when it happened.

Sean would never toss Ruhi to the side. He wanted her back in his arms right now. He didn't want Michael anywhere near her. His every instinct told him to go to her door and tell her so, to gather her back into his arms, to press his lips against hers and not let even the daylight between them.

But there was so much between them. Lies, babies, baby daddies, nightmares.

There was no way Sean could sleep. But he couldn't stay in his room with so much pent-up energy. His only choice was to leave the house.

It was just before dawn when he arrived at the stables. He saddled up one of the horses and went out for a ride. Power surged through him as he drove the horse hard, but Sean couldn't outrun his demons.

As Sean slowed the horse to a walk to cool it down, he realized he was still worked up. The ride had done nothing for his energy levels. He decided to turn his attention to some manual labor.

The sun was up now, and the inhabitants on the ranch were waking to greet the new day.

Sean looked around for something to do that wouldn't require him interacting with another person. Most of the work required another set of hands. Except the fencing.

Mending fences was best performed with another. On one's own, it proved a difficult, but doable, chore. That was precisely what Sean was looking for.

He picked up the necessary tools and set off to work. The banging of the hammer was the best therapy, especially when he imagined the nail being Michael's face. Pretty soon the sun was high on Sean's back and he heard someone approaching.

"Excuse me."

The unfamiliar voice caused Sean to stop mid-hammering. He turned to look over at the man. He was dark skinned with a well-worn face. Sean could tell the man wasn't old, a few years older than Sean possibly. But he had that aged look about him. The look of a hard life, likely once filled by drugs.

"Are you Sean Jeffries?"

"Yeah."

"I need a word with you about my son."

"Your son?"

"His name's James Ezra."

So, this was the neglectful father who couldn't be bothered to take his kid to the doctor. He'd made his way out to the ranch. But he couldn't take his kid to the pharmacy. Sean wanted a word with him too. That was why he'd called DFACS yesterday.

"I appreciate what you all are doing for my boy by bringing him out here after school," said Mr. Ezra. "What I don't appreciate is sicking child services on me. My kid needs his dad not foster care."

"He needs you to be present in his life. He needs clothes for school. He needs medication when he's sick."

Sean dropped the hammer as he approached the man. The two stood at opposite posts of the broke down fence.

"Who are you to tell me how to be a parent?"

"James has been sick for a while. You haven't done anything about it."

"I'm doing the best I can. The free clinic has a waiting list. I called when he started coughing but they couldn't give us an appointment until next month."

"He was seen here by the nurse. She gave him a prescription. It was never filled."

"What prescription?"

"We gave it to him last week. I gave him the money to get it filled."

"What money?" But no sooner than the words were out of Mr. Ezra's mouth than he closed his eyes and swore. "That's where that wad of cash came from."

Mr. Ezra pressed his lips together. He ran his hand over his brow and then over his heart. It took him a couple of tries before he could speak. It was clear the man was choked up.

"I was short on the rent this month. It's not the first time, and I thought they were finally going to evict us. But then the money showed up." Mr. Ezra choked again on the last words. "I thought I'd misplaced that money and it was my lucky day when it showed up in my drawer. But it was James."

What was he saying? Had James slipped the money Sean had slipped into his backpack into his father's dresser? Had the kid sacrificed his own health to try and help cover the bills?

"His biggest fear is going into foster care," Mr.

Ezra continued. "That could happen with an eviction. We've had Social Services watching us before. You see, I was an addict. James's mom, too. But the moment I met him, held him, I never touched another drug. I can't say the same for his mom. I'm not giving up on her. You don't give up on family. I do the best I can for him. I keep a roof over his head, food in his belly. I would've gotten him the medicine."

Sean wasn't sure what to say. His family had never had to make decisions like that one had. They never had to choose comfort over health.

"Are you a father?" asked Mr. Ezra.

Sean hesitated. Was he? The child with Ruhi was not his blood, but he felt a connection to that life growing inside her. Not just because he loved the unborn child's mother, because he'd been the first to know of the baby's existence, because he'd started making plans, because he'd altered his life for the child. Sean had stepped up, and he didn't want to back down.

"I can see you are," said Mr. Ezra. "So you understand you do what's necessary to protect your kid. I fall short on a lot of things. But I will never stop being there for him."

Sean understood that. He wasn't sure he could back away from the unborn child. He definitely wasn't backing out of his marriage.

"Listen, I'll pay you back. I don't need the charity."

"It wasn't charity," said Sean.

Mr. Ezra shook his head, but Sean held up his hand.

"The moment you stepped on this ranch you became family," said Sean. "You get no choice in the matter. Family doesn't give up on family. You just said so yourself."

Once again, Mr. Ezra's lips pressed together. He ran the back of his hand over his brow. Sean could see he was wearing the man down.

"I heard James say you're a mechanic? We've got a tractor that needs a look."

After a moment's hesitation, Mr. Ezra said, "I can take a look at it. But no family discount on the pricing."

Mr. Ezra cracked a smile as he held out his hand. Sean chuckled as he clasped the man's hand. This ranch had a way of collecting new family.

As Sean and Mr. Ezra turned to head toward the barn where the broke down tractor was parked, a

Prius drove down the lane. The man behind that wheel was not a family member that Sean wanted to collect. The car belonged to Michael.

CHAPTER TWENTY-TWO

A stabbing pain in her gut ripped Ruhi from her sleep. Her breaths came out quick and raspy. Her pulse raced, and her heartbeat thrashed in her ears. No sooner had the pain stabbed her, did it disappear entirely. What it left behind was a desolate ache in her chest.

Ruhi scratched at her chest, certain she could feel a tear. The more she rubbed, the deeper the wound felt. As a medical professional, she knew that heartbreak was real. The emotional stress caused by a breakup or stress on a relationship could appear as real, physical symptoms.

Sean had only held her for a few hours. But the loss of his arms around her, supporting her, felt like the loss of a limb. Is this what it was like to fall in love?

She'd risen to love and the ascent had been perfect. Now she'd fallen flat on her rear and it hurt worse than anything.

Sean hadn't exactly broken up with her. But his silent reproach was worse than any of the breakup lines she'd been fed. His disapproving gaze cut deeper than her parents' grimaces about her dating choices.

Ruhi did not want to live her life without his hard-earned smiles. She didn't want to walk any farther from his warm embrace. She had to figure out how to win him back.

A knock sounded at the front door. Ruhi rushed out of her bed to get it. But her steps slowed as she came into the living room.

Sean wouldn't knock on his own front door. On her bedroom door, sure. It was unlikely he lost his keys to his home. Even if he did, the inhabitants on this ranch didn't always lock doors, especially not during the day.

Ruhi didn't want to talk with anyone else. Especially if it was going to be a discussion about having one guy's baby while marrying another. Looking through the peephole, she definitely didn't want to face the man on the other side of the door. But she had to come clean.

She pulled the door open to reveal Michael.

At the sight of him standing in his collared shirt and casual slacks, Ruhi felt a dull pain in her lower back. Her heartbeat remained steady. Had her heart ever flip-flopped in his presence? She couldn't remember a single missed beat.

Michael turned on his thousand-watt smile. Ruhi squinted up at it. There was no spark. There hadn't been any chemistry between them, just compatibility.

After a moment, his smile turned to a frown, and he reared back from her. "You look awful."

She was sure she did. Her eyes were swollen from all the tears she'd cried last night. Her cheek was puffy because she'd slept on her side with her cheeks in her hands. She'd done that partly to recreate Sean's gentle touch, but also because laying on her back had become uncomfortable. And she was certain her hair was only a smidge above a rat's nest.

"You live here now?" Michael said as he came in.

Ruhi wiped a hand over her face before answering. "Yes, I just moved in the other day."

"And you're engaged?" Michael's eyes were glued to the ring on her left hand.

"Married," she confirmed.

Michael shook himself, pressing his fingers to his temples and then making an explosive gesture. "We broke up less than a week ago and you're married?"

"And pregnant." Ruhi nodded. Then she just decided to rip the Band-Aid off. "I'm six weeks pregnant."

Michael's mouth fell open. His jaw worked as though he were about to say more. Then he blinked. And blinked again.

Ruhi watched as Michael did the math in his head. She knew he'd carried the one when he took a step back from her. Just like she'd assumed he would.

There was a small part of her that had hoped he would've stepped up. Not because she wanted to be with him. Because she did want their child to have the chance to know their blood father.

"Don't worry," she said. "You don't have to have any responsibility for this baby if you don't want it. My husband is an amazing man. He will be an amazing father."

"Wait." Michael held up his hands. "Just wait a second. You're throwing all of this at me. You've known for at least a week that you're pregnant with my kid."

Well, at least he wasn't denying parentage. That gained him a point in her favor.

"You've had the time to move and get married. But not call me to let me know that I'm … I'm …?"

Michael looked from her face to her belly and back again. No matter how many times he traversed the track, he still couldn't manage to spit out his new title.

"Ruhi, this is a lot. You gotta give me at least a few minutes to process."

Michael padded from one side to the other in his leather shoes. He flicked a few glances her way, then he closed his eyes and picked up the pacing again.

Ruhi took a seat. He was obviously going to be at this for a minute. And she didn't blame him. It had taken her days to accept her condition. And that was in the midst of nausea.

Thankfully, her morning sickness had only lasted a few days. Only a dull ache remained. She was sure that would be cured once she reconciled with her husband.

But the ache was starting to get more urgent. More prickly. Almost like it was stabbing her from the inside out.

"You know, the main reason I came here was because Doctors Without Borders has been trying to reach you," said Michael. But his voice sounded far away. "You weren't answering your work or cell phone for the past few days. They reached tout o me because they knew we were colleagues. They want you too ..."

Ruhi didn't hear the rest of what Michael said. Her entire being focused in on the sharp pains radiating from her low back. Her brain had been foggy all night and morning, but as the symptoms mounted her medical brain made a clear diagnosis of what was truly happening to her.

"Ruhi?"

The pain hit her so sharply that she'd doubled over and was panting for breath. "It's the baby. Find my husband."

CHAPTER TWENTY-THREE

Sean paced up and down the tiled floors of the hospital's waiting room. Reed and Sarai sat in one set of chairs. Maggie and Eva sat across from them. They were all hunched over, worry heavy on their shoulders. Dylan, Fran, and Xavier were still at the ranch, but they checked in every half hour and planned to come over as soon as they got the chores done and the kids of the youth program back on the school bus.

Dr. and Mrs. Patel sat on a couch pushed against a wall that faced the swinging doors where the doctors had taken Ruhi over two hours ago. Where everyone on the ranch knew the score of exactly what was between him and Ruhi, her parents were still clueless. Sean had had to explain the entire situation to them, from her pregnancy to the baby's true parentage, to the arrangement he'd made with Ruhi.

He expected the Patels to be angry, upset, disappointed. They'd been surprised, most certainly. But not a single line of anger or betrayal wrinkled either of their facial features.

Dr. Patel clapped Sean on the back and then gave his shoulder a squeeze. Mrs. Patel embraced him tightly, and kissed him on his scarred cheek. Then they both retreated into the corner to wait.

Michael stood looking out a window, sneaking not so discrete glances at his watch.

Sean walked over to the man. "If there's some place you need to be, don't let us keep you."

Michael frowned as he put his hand in his pocket. "She didn't tell me, you know. I Just found out. It's a life-altering event."

Sean knew. But he hadn't hesitated when he'd figured out Ruhi's condition for himself. He'd stepped up even though it wasn't his place.

"I have other plans," Michael continued. "I'm ready to be a father. Probably ever."

At those words, Sean waited for the relief to rush through him. This would mean Michael would be out of their lives. Sean was glad for what that meant for his marriage. However, he didn't relish what that would mean for the innocent, unborn child.

"I don't want to be cast as the bad guy here," said Michael. "I'm just caught off guard and unprepared. I haven't had a chance to consider my options and make a plan."

This man was so like Ruhi with his need to arrange all the details of his life. Life didn't always work according to plan. There was that old saying after all. Sean was sure God was laughing at them both. Sean was sure He was laughing at them all.

Sean didn't mind the laughter. God could enact whatever plan he chose was best. So long as Sean got to keep the kid and the woman.

"Look," said Michael. "There's nothing between Ruhi and I. We were just casual. I mean, I'm not after her."

"Well, I am," said Sean. "I've got her. I'm not letting go. I'm holding on to the kid as well."

Something flickered in Michael's eyes. Sean wasn't sure if it was relief?

"But this is a big family," Sean continued. "There's room for you if you choose to be a part of your child's life."

Sean held out his hand. Michael stared down at it for a full minute, confusion and uncertainty on his face. Finally, the other man reached out and clasped Sean's hand. But his grip wasn't firm.

Over Michael's shoulder, Sean saw Dr. Patel smile approvingly. Sean had thought that he and Michael were far enough out of earshot that the others couldn't hear. But of course, everyone was paying attention.

"That extends to us too," said Mrs. Patel.

"Us too," said Reed.

Michael looked over at the small crowd of Ruhi's family and friends. His expression screwed in what looked like discomfort at the outpouring. This wasn't likely a part of his plan either, not this big of a family.

The double doors swung outward and the doctor who'd taken Ruhi back emerged. The white-haired woman looked down at her clipboard and not up at the group of people who rushed up to her.

"Who is the child's father?" the doctor asked.

Both Sean and Michael stepped forward. But his step was unsteady and he fell back in line with the others. Sean came to stand before the doctor.

"How's my wife?"

"She's going to be fine."

"And the baby?" asked Mrs. Patel.

"The baby is fine. Just a bit of cramping. It's not

unusual, but Mrs. Jeffries will need to stay on bed rest for a while."

"Can I see her?" asked Mrs. Patel.

"She asked to see her husband," said the doctor.

Sean heard his own footsteps as he walked down the hall to Ruhi's room. His palms were sweaty and empty. Then cold steel gripped him as he turned the doorknob.

Ruhi lay on the bed looking out the window. Her hand slid up and down her belly absentmindedly. She turned to him, and he saw a spark in her gaze. He felt it ignite his body. The door closed quietly behind him.

"Sean."

She reached for him. There was so much resonance in how she said his name. Relief, vulnerability, hope. Love.

Sean didn't hesitate. He raced to her and pulled her in his arms. "I'm so sorry for walking out on you last night."

"I should've told you about Michael. I should've told Michael about the baby. I have now."

"I know. We worked it out."

"You? We? Who?"

"Me and Michael. We agreed. I get full custody of you."

She narrowed her gaze at first. Then realization dawned. She threw back her head and laughed. The sound was like magic. It flooded his body with a warmth that made him feel safe, certain, rescued.

"He thinks he got the better deal," Sean said.

"What about the baby?" Ruhi asked.

"Worst-case scenario, this kid will have one father, half a dozen aunts, and uncles, and more people than they could ever count to care about them. This baby will want for nothing, just like his or her dad."

"I need you to know that I choose you," she said. "Over and over again, I choose you. I want to spend my life with you. I want to raise this child with you. I want to plan my life with you. I've fallen hard for you. But I don't want to do it again. It hurt. Now I just want to rise with you."

"I'm not sure what that means, but if you want it I'll give it to you."

"It means I love you."

Sean closed his eyes, savoring the sound of those words. She would be his beacon in the dark. Ruhi's light, her love. He knew he had a long way to go to manage his demons, but he now had an angel in his corner.

"I love you, too," he said, gazing down at his wife.

"I promise to reach for you and not run or walk away from you again."

Ruhi put her hand to his face. He would've sworn that her touch healed him. But his wounds had hardened on the outside. Ruhi penetrated into the depths of him, and his pulse raced to pull her close to him, to have, to hold, to protect for the rest of his days.

She was his permanent mark.

EPILOGUE

"I don't understand why we had to come all this way to buy music. Couldn't we just download it from the internet?"

Xavier sent up a silent prayer for today's youth. Kids like Carlos were so used to having everything at their fingertips with the click of a button. "I don't want a digital song. We're at this store to get the album."

Carlos' face pinched in confusion.

"You do know what an album is, don't you?"

"Yeah. It's a collection of songs that are, like, grouped together. They're in a list under an album title and you can buy them all together in one download."

All Xavier could do was shake his head. Most

kids today had never heard the scratch of a record playing, the touchdown of a needle on vinyl, the squeak is a part of the record skipped. They heard everything as a pristine replication of ones and zeros, no analogous waves.

"Whoa, this looks like something out of an old-time movie," said Carlos.

Xavier put his truck in park outside of the small mom and pop record store. It was one of the last in the entire state, likely one of few remaining in the entire United States. Just like independent bookstores and home movie stores, music stores were disappearing fast in the modern world of online retail, subscription services, and free downloads.

Xavier wasn't entirely averse to the digital takeover. It made getting the obscure music he liked to listen to easier. He had a healthy iTunes library of purchased music. There was a library of CDs in his home. But Xavier was a traditionalist in this sense. When he could get the physical album, he'd jump at the chance. Even if that meant driving an hour out of his way to do so.

He hopped out and went into the one-story building. On the right of the record store was a small diner with very few customers. On the left was an electronics store. Unfortunately, all the lights were off inside. It had likely gone out of business some time ago as handheld devices took over the technological world.

Inside the record store, a pretty woman stood behind the counter. She had earbuds in her ears and was looking down at the cell phone. She didn't look up as he came up to the counter.

"Excuse me?"

She didn't respond and he had to repeat himself twice, getting louder each time. When he finally caught her attention, her brows pinched in annoyance. Until they landed on his face. Then the telltale smile of interest lit her features.

Xavier was used to women showing interest in him based on his looks. He would've distracted himself with her attention, but for the long drive, and the preteen browsing the aisles.

"I called ahead," he said. "You should be holding an album for me. Songs of Faith by Aretha Franklin."

She went behind the counter and came back with the album. "Is it for your mom?"

"No."

Xavier didn't offer more. He reached out for the album with greedy hands. He'd been searching for this for years and finally, he had it in his hands again.

"It's over a hundred dollars for this," said the clerk. "You know you could get it for ten bucks on Amazon."

Xavier jerked his gaze up to her, disgust clear on his face. What was she doing working in a record shop if she pushed people to the competitor? It didn't matter. He'd found what he was looking for and now it was time to go.

But after paying, he couldn't bring himself to leave immediately. There was something about a record store and the musty way it smelled. He found joy flipping through albums looking for a treasure. It reminded him of his youth and his time with...

He shook his head. He didn't think about that time. Or her. Those memories were all in the past. Perhaps he should go back and talk to the disloyal cashier. She was so unlike her that it would certainly take his mind off of his past.

Carlos had found the sheet music section and was busy looking for the notes to Final Fantasy. He'd recently joined the school band. The kid had settled on drums to the dismay of all the early-rising residents of the ranch.

Xavier looked up at the cashier. Yeah, she might

be a good distraction for a few minutes. Just remind him of how much he'd changed since his younger years. How much he didn't deserve a girl in a floral dress who smelled of lilacs blowing in the wind.

Xavier took a step towards the clerk but there was something tethered to his leg. He looked down to find a child with her stubby arms wrapped around his right leg.

"Sorry," said the cashier. "That's the other cashier's kid. She doesn't speak. She usually doesn't even interact with people."

Xavier stared down at the child. She had a round face, like the cherubs on the stained glass windows of his hometown church. She smiled up at him with the most angelic grin. But it was her eyes that caught and held him. They were steel gray with royal blue at the edges. It was like he was looking in a mirror.

In the distance, he heard a door open. Voices trailed out. One of the voices was filled with distress, but the tone of it was so familiar it brought memories he'd long tried to bury back to the surface. Xavier inhaled to push them away and the smell of lilacs on the wind nearly knocked him over.

"I'm sorry, Mr. Adams. It won't happen again. I'm looking for a new sitter for Alex now and... Alex? Alex?"

The little girl let go of Xavier's leg and raced over to the woman calling out frantically. Once the woman saw the child, she breathed a sigh of relief and scooped the little girl into her arms.

"Alexandra where did you go? I told you to sit in the chair until mommy was finished her meeting."

Alex grinned and pointed to Xavier who was only standing because he was leaning against the rack of records. The sigh of relief that had just left the woman's mouth turned into a gasp of dismay when she met Xavier's gaze.

"Xavier?"

"Cassie?"

He wasn't sure if he said her name aloud. It had been over two years since he'd uttered the name of his first and only love. Nearly five since he'd last seen her.

And now she was standing in front of him. Holding the hand of a child who couldn't have been more than four. A child who had his eyes.

Can you say secret baby?
You won't want to miss Purple Heart Ranch's notorious bad boy reconnect with the good girl who got away. Even

more importantly, you won't want to miss why these two had to part ways. And then witness their journey back to each other.

That's what's coming up next in the next installment in
Having His Back
Book Five of The Brides of Purple Heart Ranch.

Order your copy today!

Shanae Johnson was raised by Saturday Morning cartoons and After School Specials. She still doesn't understand why there isn't a life lesson that ties the issues of the day together just before bedtime. While she's still waiting for the meaning of it all, she writes stories to try and figure it all out. Her books are wholesome and sweet, but her are heroes are hot and heroines are full of sass!

And by the way, the E elongates the A. So it's pronounced Shan-aaaaaaaa. Perfect for a hero to call out across the moors, or up to a balcony, or to blare outside her window on a boombox. If you hear him calling her name, please send him her way!

You can sign up for Shanae's Reader Group at http://bit.ly/ShanaeJohnsonReaders

Also By Shanae Johnson

The Brides of Purple Heart

On His Bended Knee

Hand Over His Heart

Offering His Arm

His Permanent Scar

Having His Back

In Over His Head

Always On His Mind

Every Step He Takes

In His Good Hands

Light Up His Life

Strength to Stand

The Rangers of Purple Heart

The Rancher takes his Convenient Bride

The Rancher takes his Best Friend's Sister

The Rancher takes his Runaway Bride

The Rancher takes his Star Crossed Love

The Rancher takes his Love at First Sight

The Rancher takes his Last Chance at Love

The Rebel Royals series

The King and the Kindergarten Teacher

The Prince and the Pie Maker

The Duke and the DJ

The Marquis and the Magician's Assistant

The Princess and the Principal

The Marquis and the Magician's Assistant

The Princess and the Principal